SWING A WIDE LOOP

LESLIE SCOTT

THORNDIKE
CHIVERS

This Large Print edition is published by Thorndike Press, Waterville, Maine, USA and by AudioGO Ltd, Bath, England.
Thorndike Press, a part of Gale, Cengage Learning.
The text of this Large Print edition is unabridged.
Other aspects of the book may vary from the original edition.
Set in 16 pt. Plantin.
Printed on permanent paper.

LIBRARY OF CONGRESS CATALOGING-IN-PUBLICATION DATA

Scott, Leslie, 1893–1975.
    Swing a wide loop / by Leslie Scott. — Large print ed.
      p. cm. — (Thorndike Press large print western)
    ISBN-13: 978-1-4104-2356-6 (alk. paper)
    ISBN-10: 1-4104-2356-5 (alk. paper)
    1. Fort Worth (Tex.)—Fiction. 2. Large type books. I. Title.
PS3537.C9265S95 2010
813'.54—dc22   2009049089

BRITISH LIBRARY CATALOGUING-IN-PUBLICATION DATA AVAILABLE

Published in 2010 in the U.S. by arrangement with Golden West Literary Agency.
Published in 2010 in the U.K. by arrangement with Golden West Literary Agency.

U.K. Hardcover: 978 1 408 49086 0 (Chivers Large Print)
U.K. Softcover: 978 1 408 49087 7 (Camden Large Print)

Printed and bound in Great Britain by
CPI Antony Rowe, Chippenham, Wiltshire
1 2 3 4 5 6 7 14 13 12 11 10 09

SWING A WIDE LOOP

CHAPTER ONE

The prairie lay drenched in sunshine. The grassheads rippled like the waves of a languid sea. Sunshine and peace, save for one dark cloud that rolled steadily from the south.

Lightning-like flashes accompanied that rolling cloud; and a low rumble as of distant thunder. The flashes were sunlight flung back from a myriad tossing horns. The thunder was the steady beat of a myriad hoofs. Like an ominous promise of doom overdue, the trail herd rolled northward. The longhorns were on the march again, and the trails of Texas were flinging their last challenge to the ever-advancing ribbons of steel.

Jim Wayne, riding with the drag, gazed across three thousand shaggy backs and had a premonition that this was the last really great drive to flow northward over the Texas trails. The Forked S shipping herd was one of the five booming to the Red River and across the plains of Oklahoma and Kansas to Dodge City, Kansas, and the railroad. Far to the front, out of sight for the time being, were the Cross C, the Rafter, the Y Bench and the Walking R. All would pause at Fort Worth to rest and graze the weary cows before the next ninety-mile-long leg to the Red. More than fifteen thousand rambunctious longhorns bawled and rumbled their protests at the hoof-wearing journey to death.

Old Lafe Swanson, the Forked S owner, came riding back along the marching column to confer with his young range boss.

'What you doing back here eating dust?' he asked, fanning some of it away with his hat.

Wayne glanced back at the remuda of spare horses following the cattle, and the chuck wagon rumbling along still farther behind.

'Just wanted to make sure everything is in shape to hit town,' he replied. 'I think I'll send the wagon on ahead, so Pete can have something to eat ready by the time we get bedded down. If everyone is as hungry as I am, the boys will be hankering for a surrounding by then.'

'You young fellers!' snorted Swanson. 'All

you think of is eating or women. When you get to be my age you'll settle for a few snorts of red-eye and a spell of pounding your ear.'

'Oh, we won't pass up the red-eye,' Wayne returned cheerfully. 'It lays a good foundation for eating or anything else.'

Swanson chuckled. 'Maybe you got something there,' he admitted. 'Hope they'll be able to tell us at Fort Worth how the Old Red is acting up.'

'I can tell you how it's going to be acting up when we get there next week,' Wayne predicted grimly. 'It's going to be in flood or close to it. There's rain up to the northwest, or all signs fail. In fact, I wouldn't be surprised if we get some down here; the barometer is falling.'

Old Lafe snorted again. 'You educated fellers! You go by a thingamajig hung in the wagon. I know there's rain coming when I smell it.'

'Doubtless your olfactory nerves are more sensitive than mine.' Wayne smiled. 'All I can smell is cow.'

They reined in to let the chuck wagon come abreast of them. Wayne fished out the makings and deftly rolled a cigarette with the fingers of his left hand. Old Lafe worried off a chaw from a plug of eating tobacco and regarded his range boss.

He saw a tall man, over six feet, with wide shoulders and a deep chest slimming down to a lean, sinewy waist. And around that supple waist were double cartridge-belts from the holsters of which protruded the plain black butts of heavy guns. Everybody packed a gun, sometimes two, but somehow those Colt Forty-fives seemed a part of Jim Wayne.

'His dad packed guns that way,' Swanson reminded himself. 'Old Preston Wayne was mighty fast on the draw, but there are folks who say young Jim could shade him. Don't think he's ever had to use those irons, but if he ever does —'

Jim Wayne had crisp, thick black hair over a wide forehead. Under heavy black brows, his eyes were rather long, level and pale grey in colour. He had a prominent hawk nose, lean, deeply bronzed cheeks and a powerful chin and jaw. His mouth, rather wide and good-humoured, modified the sternness of his countenance.

The remuda shambled past, the wrangler in charge whooping a cheery greeting. Along came the chuck wagon, driven by a bristly individual of uncertain age and uncertain temper. He bawled profane acquiescence to Wayne's order, swerved his horses and sent them surging ahead, well to the left of the cows; stampedes had been started by less.

'Old Pete's been with me nigh on to forty years,' Swanson observed reminiscently. 'Was *old* Pete back in those days, too. He's a hundred and seventy-five years old if he's a day.'

'Knock off a hundred of that and you'll about hit it,' Wayne replied. 'But no matter how old he is, he sure can cook, regardless of circumstances or conditions. He could light a fire under a waterfall.' Swanson chuckled, and didn't argue.

'Guess we'd better circle around and get ahead of the herd,' he said. 'May have trouble finding a good bedding down patch, with those outfits ahead of us.' Wayne nodded, and they sent their horses ahead at a fast pace.

The herd was not grazing along in a great arrowhead formation, point to the front, but jostled briskly in a long column, for Wayne wanted to reach the vicinity of Fort Worth before dark fell. The cows didn't like it, but had no choice in the matter.

A third of the way ahead of the drag they passed the flank riders, who rode in pairs on either side of the herd to block any tendency to wander sideways and to drive off any foreign cattle that sought to join the herd.

Another third of the way ahead, and they waved to the swing riders, who were stationed where the herd began to bend.

Riding a third of the way back from the head of the column were the point riders. Were a change of direction desired, each would ride abreast of the foremost cattle, then quietly veer in the desired direction. The lead cows would swerve away from the rider approaching them and towards the one who was receding.

The most skilled and dependable hands were chosen for point, the honoured post of the drive and the one of greatest responsibility, for the point men had to determine the exact direction the range boss desired the herd to take.

Nobody rode directly in front of the herd, whose leader was always some wary and trailwise old steer who took over of his own accord. He was an invaluable beast, sometimes so valuable that he was retained when the herd was disposed of, taken back to the home pasture, given a name and help in readiness to 'captain' the next shipping herd to take the trail.

The particular critter attached to the Forked S outfit was possessed of uncanny wisdom, and this was far from the first time he had led the northern trek. Jim Wayne had named him Casanova, and he lived up to his name.

Having made sure everything was in order, Wayne and old Lafe rode on. The range boss gestured to a dark smudge fouling the clean blue of the northern sky.

'Smoke of Fort Worth,' he observed. 'We'll make it in good time.'

'Been a mighty good drive so far,' remarked Swanson. 'Jim, you sure know how to handle 'em.'

'Worst part is still to come,' Wayne replied. 'But maybe we'll make out.'

'I ain't worried,' declared old Lafe. 'Will sure hate to lose you when you tie on to a spread of your own, as you figure to do, but I don't blame you. I know how you feel about working for wages all your life, like so many of the boys do, and I'll lend you all the help I can.'

'Thanks, Uncle Lafe,' Wayne said. 'So far, though, I haven't been able to swing anything. I'd hoped to stay in the Nueces River country with you, but folks hang on to their holdings there, and those who might consider selling for some reason or other ask a price way beyond what I can afford to pay.'

'Something will turn up,' Swanson replied. 'You may get a surprise all of a sudden.'

'Maybe,' Wayne conceded, but without

13

enthusiasm. 'I'm afraid, though, I'll have to go farther afield to find something within my means. Might try the Big Bend or west of the Pecos.'

'Rough country over there,' Swanson commented.

'No rougher than right here and what's liable to develop here,' Wayne differed. 'A section is only as rough as the people in it, and there are plenty pouring in here right now, and a lot more to come, of all sorts. Take Fort Worth, for example. More than five thousand people there now, and just a few years back there was hardly anybody except some trappers. Then the trail herds coming up from the south caused it to grow. And with the railroad headed this way, she's booming. Land values are going up, new buildings being constructed. Time will come when Fort Worth will be the centre of the livestock industry of the South-west, and the devil only knows what else will develop here. And as I said, the boom is and will be bringing in all sorts. Liable to be about as rough as anywhere before long. I sure wish I'd been able to get in on the ground floor here before things really started moving. With the coming of the Texas and Pacific Railroad, Fort Worth and the surrounding section is in for real prosperity. Fine rangeland to the west, the beginning of the North Central Plains. And the Grand Prairie to the east will be fine for farming and fruit growing.'

'Could be,' Swanson admitted, and the subject was dropped.

Without incident, the trail herd boomed into the environs of Fort Worth. There was plenty of time to bed down, plenty of good pasture on the prairie to the west, and sufficient water. So the chore of bedding down for the night was completed before sundown, and the hands gathered around the chuck wagon for much needed food.

While they were eating, Frank Carter, owner of the Cross C, the first outfit to reach Fort Worth, rode in with news.

'Just come from town,' he announced. 'Pueblo's in a dither for fair. They'd figured on a railroad soon, and things have been arranged accordingly. Yep, they figured on a real boom, but looks like they figured wrong. They ain't got no railroad, and don't look like they'll have one soon, if ever.'

'How's that?' Wayne asked.

'Well,' replied Carter, 'the railroad has reached Eagle Ford, not much more than twenty-five miles from Fort Worth. But the word came through last week that Jay Cook and Company has gone bust along with a lot of other concerns over East. The Jay Cook people held most of the liens against the new railroad, the Texas and Pacific, and also against a lot of property in Fort Worth. Folks there are plumb scared and have already started pulling out. Betcha that in a couple of months there won't be a thousand people left, and right now better than five thousand are squatting there. The bottom's dropped out of land values, including range-land, and everybody is anxious to sell, with no takers. It's a mess.'

'Yes, looks like it is,' Wayne agreed, his eyes thoughtful. 'You figure there's no chance of the road coming through soon?'

'Or ever, according to what folks keep saying,' Carter replied. 'Well, I'm sorry for the folks here, but it ain't any concern of ours. This patch is just a bedding down spot and a chance to lay in chuck and other stuff we'll need.'

'It would make a difference to us if the railroad actually did come through, though,' Wayne pointed out. 'Chances are we'd use it for a shipping point rather than make the long drive to Kansas.'

'Uh-huh, you got something there,' Carter conceded.

'There's another angle that's got folks bothered,' he resumed. 'Seems there was a

16

land grant subsidy given by the legislature that set a time limit on the road's construction, and if that grant is allowed to expire there'll be mighty small chance of getting another, with a row busting loose about too many grants having been given to the railroads. And no land grant subsidy will mean no railroad for Fort Worth. Instead, the roads will build to the south where they've got grants.'

'But if the road is pushed through to Fort Worth before the grant expires it holds good?' Wayne asked.

'So I understand,' Carter replied. 'But nobody 'pears overly hopeful of that happening. And the way folks are leaving, looks like there won't be nobody here before long to care one way or other.'

'Some will stay,' Wayne said with conviction. 'I've a notion quite a few folks are going to try to fight this thing to a finish; that's the Texas way, and there must be quite a few Texans here.'

'Guess there are,' Carter admitted. 'But the town's changed a heap since I was here last, three years back. A lot more saloons, and I noticed some tough-looking customers in them. I let all my boys except the night guard go to town for a little bust, but I told 'em to stick together.'

'I'll tell mine the same,' Swanson put in. 'You'd better go along, Jim, and keep an eye on them.'

CHAPTER TWO

Wayne jogged along Fort Worth's Main Street to what would later be called Tenth Street and drew rein at a hitchrack opposite a plate glass window on which a dispenser of beverages with a poetic strain had legended 'The Western Star'. He had visited the Western Star on a previous drive, and he and the Forked S hands had agreed it was okay as saloons went and better than most. He reasoned that here he would find most if not all of his hands partaking of something to wash the dust from their throats.

Wayne dismounted and dropped the split reins to the ground, knowing that was all that was necessary to keep Flame, the sorrel, in place.

'You take it easy, now,' Wayne told him. 'An extra helpin' of oats in the nose-bag when we get back to camp.'

Flame tried out the hitchrack bar with his

teeth, gave it a shake, decided it was satisfactory and relapsed into what appeared a comatose condition.

Wayne chuckled. Flame would be right there when wanted, and if anybody tried to lay a hand on him it would be at the risk of losing the hand and perhaps part of an arm along with it. Flame was a 'one-man' horse.

The poetic vendor of that harmless beverage known as straight whisky was a gentleman who had attained an altitude of six feet and a little more and a waistline circumference of almost the same and who rejoiced in the elegant sobriquet of Sweatless Sam.

Wayne liked Sweatless Sam, and the regard was reciprocated. Sam spotted him the instant he pushed his way through the swinging doors and hurried to greet him, hand outstretched, smiles wreathing his rubicund features, his step singularly quick and light for so huge a man.

'Well! well!' he bellowed in a voice that caused the hanging lamps to jump. 'How are you, Jim? Plumb glad to see you. I figured you'd show up soon and kept a table over in the corner, so we could have a quiet drink together. Your boys are all here, having a high old time. Come on and take a load off your feet.'

They shook hands warmly and repaired to

the table, which was near the dance floor. Sweatless beckoned a waiter.

'Private stock,' he said. 'Only the best for my old *amigo*. Headed for Dodge City again, eh, Jim?'

'Yep, a big one this time,' Wayne replied as they raised their glasses. He glanced about, studying the crowded room.

The Western Star was hopping, all right, but Wayne noted certain tight groups that conversed soberly and took no part in the general hilarity. These, he gathered, were townspeople, with a sprinkling of ranch owners. He looked questioningly at Sweatless.

'Well, what do you think about it?'

'What do *you* think?' Sweatless countered.

'I think,' Wayne said slowly, 'that after this flurry is over, Fort Worth is going to grow bigger and better than ever before. And I also think,' he added, 'that Fort Worth will get its railroad if folks will just rise up and stir their stumps.'

Sweatless nodded sagely. 'I feel the same way about it,' he replied. 'Plenty of folks don't, and they're pulling out. Me, I'm going to stay right where I am. I figure to weather the storm and haul in the chips sooner or later.'

'Right,' Wayne said. 'I feel so certain of it

21

that I aim to invest in a spread hereabouts, if I can grab off one at a reasonable price.'

'Oh, you can grab off one, all right,' Sweatless returned. 'No trouble about that. Everybody is anxious to sell, except some smart folks who know better. You can just about name your price.'

'All right,' Wayne said. 'Do me a favour, will you, Sam? Keep your eyes open and see if you can line up something by the time I get back from Dodge City. It will give you a few weeks to look around.'

'I'll do it,' Sweatless promised. 'I always figured you for a smart hombre, Jim. Now I know I figured right. We'll show these paper-backed gents a thing or two before we're finished. Waiter, fill 'em up again; we'll drink to it.'

They raised their glasses again, grinning at each other.

'Yes, sir,' Wayne said. 'We're going to get our railroad and have a real ripsnorter of a town here even if every bank and peanut stand in the whole blasted East fails.'

'My sentiments exactly,' said Sweatless. 'Let us drink!'

While the waiter was filling the glasses, Sweatless studied the crowded room and his heavy brows drew together.

'The scavengers are already beginning to show up,' he remarked. 'They always do at a time like this; they have the buzzard's scent for pickings. You see, strange though it may seem, everything considered, folks are packing a lot more money than usual. They're drawing it from the bank, those that figure to move. Others who figure to stay see nice bargains of various sorts to be picked up, so they are heeled to take advantage of opportunities. And everybody is keyed up with a reckless feeling. All of which works to the advantage of the owl-hoot brand. Right now I see quite a few we could do without. Don't know 'em, and don't want to. But I'm keeping my eyes open in case they start something in here. Don't think they will, but you never can tell.'

Wayne nodded. He had already noted several gentlemen of the sort that preferred to do their riding during the hours between sunset and sunrise. They dressed like cow-hands and probably had been once, but he suspected that they had no recent marks of rope or branding-iron on their hands.

He had been watching the steady flow of new arrivals pushing through the swinging doors. They were for the most part average and ordinary individuals, but some stood

23

out. This applied strongly to a man who entered at that moment. He was tall, with almost cameo-perfect features, tawny hair worn rather long and, in contrast to his blond colouring, eyes that were black, with a quick glitter in their depths. He glanced about, waved a hand to Sweatless Sam and made his way to the bar.

'That's Malcolm Otey from Dallas,' said Sweatless. 'He seems to be a pretty nice feller, and an up-and-coming jigger, too. He's been buying land around Dallas. Has a real estate office there. Writes articles for the Dallas newspaper. 'Pears to have a finger in a lot of pies. It was him brought the word from Dallas that Jay Cook and Company had gone bust and that the railroad had stopped building at Eagle Ford.'

Wayne nodded, and regarded Malcolm Otey with interest. A fine-looking man, all right, and one who gave the impression of being able and adroit. He wore a long black coat, dark striped trousers and shiny boots. The snow of his ruffled shirt-front brightened his sombre attire, and against it his string tie was startlingly black in contrast. His hat also was black, new and neatly creased.

'Almost like a gambler's rig,' Wayne commented.

'Guess he is one, in a way,' said Sam. 'Buying and selling land is a good deal of a gamble, even more so than cards. You can sorta figure the cards sometimes, but real estate! You never know which way the cat is going to jump. Look at Fort Worth right now. Same thing, somehow or other, could happen to Dallas. Yep, Otey's a gambler, all right, only I don't figure he goes in for the pasteboards. Too slow for the likes of him.'

Suddenly Sweatless gave a disgusted snort. 'And here comes one we could well do without, Ran Ellis, and some of his hellions.'

Ran Ellis was also a big man. He was not as tall as Malcolm Otey but more heavily built. He walked with a swagger, swinging his thick shoulders truculently, as if his motto were — 'Get out of my way!' His craggy, big-nosed face was dominated by hot blue eyes that seemed never still, continually shooting glances to all parts of the room. Unlike the impeccably garbed Otey, his rangeland clothes were the worse for wear. His Levi's — bibless overalls — were wrinkled and stuffed into scuffed boots. His blue shirt, open at the throat, was streaked with sweat, his broad-brimmed 'J.B.' battered. His four companions, lean, alert-looking men, were similarly dressed, and all

25

five needed a shave.

'Look like they've just come off the range and a hard day's work,' Wayne commented.

'Uh-huh, off somebody's range,' Sweatless grunted.

'He's an owner?' Wayne asked. Sweatless nodded.

'Has a little spread down to the south, the Boxed B, not far from the Big Bottoms. Has a lot of cows for so little a spread.'

Wayne regarded his companion curiously. 'What you driving at?' he asked. 'Just what is wrong with him?'

Sweatless shrugged his big shoulders. 'Well, for one thing he's a trouble maker. He'll pick a fight at the drop of a hat, and is plumb willing to drop it himself if nobody else will oblige. Some folks 'low his herd grows too fast. As to that I don't know. Other things said about him, but I ain't passing 'em on. Could be doing the feller an injustice. The loco coloured folks, some of 'em, say — but they don't say it very loud — that he's Cullen Barnet come back to life.'

'Cullen Barnet?'

'That's right — the worst outlaw this section ever knew. The Texas Rangers were supposed to have killed him in the Big Bottoms, but nobody ever was plumb sure about that. Anyhow, he was shot and fell in the Black Water, a big creek there full of 'gators and snakes and snags and trailing vines, that nobody ever went into and come out alive. Coloured folks say Cullen came out alive, though. Say he was bad hurt, but that an old cunjer woman who lives in the Bottoms and weaves spells and makes root medicine put him in shape and that he left the section for a while but now he's come back. I don't take any stock in such a yarn, but the hellion does sort of answer to Cullen Barnet's description according to old-timers. Only nobody can remember Barnet having a big scar alongside his left eye like Ellis has. Coloured folks have something to say about that, too. Say he got that scar swimming the Black Water; that the Devil put his mark on him so he'd know him when he wanted him.'

Wayne chuckled. 'Quite a yarn. Sort of like some of the Nueces River country stories of the Men of Steel, the old Spanish conquerors come back to life, or Ol' Coffin-head, the giant rattlesnake, "who's got so old he's done growed whiskers." '

Sweatless nodded. 'Uh-huh, Texas is full of such yarns. What with Mexicans and coloured people, and folks from across the Pond who bring Old Country legends and myths and superstitions with them when they come to America and land in Texas, you can hear 'most anything.'

'Entertaining but not to be taken too seriously,' Wayne said. 'I imagine the Cullen Barnet yarns are out of the whole cloth. Notorious outlaws are always coming to life. There are folks who will tell you that Jesse James is living in Texas right now.'

Nevertheless, he studied Ran Ellis with quickened interest.

One of Ellis's riders interested him even more than Ellis himself. He was very tall and very thin, with abnormally long arms. His bony, muscular hands, dangling loosely by his sides, reminded Wayne of spear-points. His face, very dark, was cadaverous, running to a great beak of a nose. His eyes were a muddy-looking brown, his mouth a thin line like the gash of a raw wound, almost reptilian in appearance. His movements were slow but precise and sure. He wore two guns low on his thighs. Indian blood, Wayne concluded. Very like Apache.

'Who's the snake on stilts?' he asked.

'That's Val Rader, Ellis's range boss,' Sweatless replied. 'Mean-looking cuss, ain't he?'

'I've a notion he can take care of himself,' Wayne conceded.

28

Sweatless ordered another drink. 'They're chortling over at Dallas,' he observed. 'They look on Fort Worth as a rival, especially where the cattle trade is concerned. The cowmen have gotten used to making the long drive to Abilene or Dodge City in Kansas, and they're slow to change, but they'll come to it sooner or later and ship from this section. Dallas figures on grabbing all that trade once a railroad line from the East gets to them. Looked like Fort Worth was going to get the line; but now they figure what's happened just about eliminates her.'

'They may get a surprise,' Wayne commented. 'With the trails running as they do, Fort Worth is the better shipping point.'

'If Fort Worth manages to get something to ship with,' Sweatless replied with a touch of pessimism.

'Fort Worth will,' Wayne declared definitely.

'Hope you're right, and somehow I've a notion you are, although things don't look too good right now,' Sweatless said. 'Well, I reckon after I finish this snort I'd better circulate around a bit and see how things are going. The herds will roll in the morning, eh? I'll have something good spotted for you by the time you get back from

29

Kansas.'

'Thanks,' Wayne replied. 'I think I'll join my boys at the bar, to keep an eye on them; the red-eye will be buzzing in their ears before long. Be seeing you.' 🌿

Wayne had almost reached the bar when he stepped on a wet cigar-butt that slid under his foot. He lurched forward, off balance, and slammed into Ran Ellis, who was just raising a brimming glass to his lips. Ellis got the glass against his teeth, the whisky in his face. He gave a roar of anger and whirled around.

'You blankety-blank clumsy range tramp!' he bellowed, and swung a blow at Wayne's face.

It didn't land. Wayne moved his head slightly, and the big fist whizzed over his shoulder. Ellis drew back his left hand, and Wayne hit him. Ellis sat down on the floor, hard.

Sweatless Sam came rushing forward, shouting protests.

'Let him alone,' Wayne snapped. 'He needs a lesson, and he's going to get it.'

Ellis let out another roar. 'I'll lesson you!' He bounced off the floor like a rubber ball and rushed, both fists swinging.

Cowhands, as a rule, know little of the

manly art of self-defence. Jim Wayne, however, knew considerably more than a little; he had done quite a bit of boxing when attending college. He measured his man coolly as Ellis bounded towards him.

Just the same, Wayne knew he had a fight on his hands. Ellis outweighed him by more than thirty pounds and he was built like a granite block. A sizzling left hook gashed the rancher's cheek bone. An uppercut checked but did not stop him. He came on, swinging right and left. One of those wild haymakers got past Wayne's guard and caught him on the chin, snapping his head back and slamming him against the bar. Ellis whooped with triumph, leaped forward for the kill and met a straight right that staggered him. He ducked his head, took a blow on top of it, and flung his blocky arms around Wayne.

'He's got the under holt!' somebody shouted. 'That cowboy's done for!'

He wasn't. Jim Wayne also knew something of wrestling. His cupped hands came up under Ellis's chin, with all his two hundred pounds of sinewy weight behind them. Ellis's head went back, more and more. He wrestled mightily to throw Wayne off his feet, but that deadly pressure was more than his cervical vertebrae could stand. He loosened his hold and staggered free. And Wayne hit him, square and true, on the angle of the jaw. Ellis was lifted clear off his feet. He hit the floor with a crash and stayed there, writhing and jerking.

In one unbroken ripple of movement, Jim Wayne's hands flashed down and up. The hanging lamps jumped to the boom of a shot.

CHAPTER THREE

Val Rader, the Boxed E range boss, gave a howl of pain and gripped his blood-spurting hand between his knees. The gun he had drawn, one butt-plate knocked off, lay on the floor a dozen feet distant.

Jim Wayne had a gun in each hand. The black muzzles, one wisping smoke, were trained on the Boxed E riders. They flinched under their menace.

'Anybody else have the notion of fanging?' Wayne asked, his voice brittle.

From the floor came an indignant bellow. Ran Ellis was sitting up, rubbing his swelling jaw.

'What's the shooting about?' he wanted to know 'Has somebody gone loco?'

Wayne gestured to the cursing Rader and holstered his guns. Ellis lumbered to his feet.

'Val, why the blankety-blank-blank do you always have to go off half cocked?' he demanded in injured tones. 'This gent and me were just having a sociable little wring. We didn't mean each other any harm.'

'I thought he'd killed you,' mumbled Rader.

'Well, he didn't,' Ellis replied. 'There was nothing to get on the prod about.'

Sweatless Sam pushed his way to the front. 'Come on to the back room, Val, and I'll tie up your lunch hook,' he said. 'Just a scratch.'

As he started to follow the saloon-keeper, Rader turned to Wayne, a grudging admiration in his eyes. 'Feller, you're fast, real fast,' he said. He picked up his damaged gun and lurched away after Sweatless.

'He ain't overly bright, but he's got the loyalty of a dog,' Ellis said. 'Sorta feels beholden to me, I reckon. I pulled him from in front of a stampede once, and he made a big thing of it.'

'And came darned near getting yourself killed doing it,' observed one of the Boxed E hands. 'That's how he got that scar alongside his head,' he added to Wayne.

'You're a liar,' Ellis said cheerfully. 'I got that shaving.'

'Here comes the marshal!' somebody shouted.

The town marshal, a grizzled and lanky

old-timer, eyed the gathering with dis-
approval.

'All right, who got plugged?' he demanded. 'I heard the shooting.'

'Shooting?' Ran Ellis's eyes were wide and
innocent. 'Marshal, you must be imagining
things. There wasn't any shooting. This gent
and me were going to have a bottle of
champagne together, and when the drink
juggler turned it over, the darned thing blew
up.'

The marshal did not appear impressed.
'I'll padlock this blasted rum hole sooner or
later, see if I don't,' he grumbled.

'Might as well,' said Ellis. 'Looks like
everything else is going to be padlocked,
come this time next month. Barkeep, drop
a loop on another bottle, and be sure this
one don't blow up.'

'Yes, be darn sure this one don't blow us,'
the marshal said significantly, and walked
out.

'He's okay,' chuckled Ellis. 'A bad jigger
to start trouble with, but he don't bother
anybody if he doesn't have to. Feller, you're
good. The last one you handed me was a
lulu. I'd like to have another go with you
sometime; I want you to show me that one-
two shift you used.'

'Be glad to,' replied Wayne.

The grinning bartender had supplied a bottle of champagne. 'I'll put it in the tub to cool,' he said. 'Then maybe it won't blow up.'

'Fine,' said Ellis. 'Feller,' he added to Wayne, 'my name's Ellis, Ran Ellis. I don't believe I caught your handle.'

Wayne supplied it, and they shook hands. Ellis rattled off the names of the three punchers, who ducked their heads and grinned.

'Yes, that last one was a lulu,' he repeated. 'I saw stars and comets and all kinds of real purty lights; but I don't want to see any more.'

Before the bottle was cool, Val Rader, his hand bandaged, returned.

'Give this gent your left and tell him you're sorry,' Ellis ordered.

Rader stuck out his bony hand, which Wayne accepted. He grinned, and suddenly his cadaverous face did not look so sinister.

'I'm sorry, feller,' he said. 'I sorta cotton to the Boss,' he added, as if that were all the explanation necessary.

'Here comes the bubble water,' said Ellis. 'Suppose those gents behind you who had their irons out and ready to back your play are your boys, eh? Bring 'em here and we'll all have a snort. That's a big bottle, and there ought to be enough to go around. If there isn't, we'll tie on to another one.'

The half-dozen Forked S punchers moved closer, and there was a general handshaking and tossing about of names.

'I don't care much for this stuff,' said Ellis, raising his glass, 'but it sorta seems the right thing for celebrating a nice ruckus like we had. Suppose you're with one of those herds bedded down over to the west of town?'

'That's right,' Wayne admitted. 'The Forked S.'

'Good!' said Ellis. 'Looks like we'll get a chance to see more of each other. I'm running a herd to Dodge City and figured to trail along behind you fellers. The more the better, the way things are up around the Red and in Kansas. The bigger the bunch, the less chance of running into trouble. Figure this will be the last one I run north.'

'Going to pull out of the section?' Wayne asked. Ellis shook his head.

'Aim to stay,' he replied. 'I figure this to be an up-and-coming section, despite all the hullabaloo and what folks are saying. Fort Worth's going to be okay, especially if we can just figure a way to finagle that railroad. Only a bit over twenty-five miles from here right now. Don't tell me that folks back East are going to give up that easy. Things like this have happened before, and the country always managed to come out of it. Will do it again. Yes, I've got faith in Fort Worth. What do you think?'

'I think you've got the right notion,' Wayne replied.

'Good,' said Ellis. 'Maybe you might decide to coil your twine in the section,' he added hopefully. 'If you do, there's a job of riding for you. I can use a feller like you, and maybe if you're hanging around I can figure a way to lick you.' He bellowed with laughter.

'If that one you landed on my chin had been just a little more to the left, you wouldn't have to be bothering about it.' Wayne smiled.

Ellis shook his head dubiously. 'Wouldn't want to bet on it,' he disagreed. 'You were riding with the punch, something I've never learned to do right. I'm like an old short-horn bull — I duck my head and charge.'

'Never a wise thing to do with a big man who can hit,' Wayne replied. 'Nobody can take a really solid one on the jaw and stay on his feet.'

'Huh! Don't I know it, after tonight,' Ellis said dryly. 'You think you might possibly drift up this way again?'

'I expect I'll be back,' Wayne replied, without committing himself further.

'Good!' repeated Ellis. 'Be glad to have you. Say, I think Sweatless is trying to catch your eye; he's over there at the table with that feller Otey from Dallas. We'll be going now; got a busy day ahead of us. See you tomorrow.'

'Come on, boys, call it a night,' he told his hands. They trooped out.

Wayne moved to the table where Otey and the saloon-keeper sat. Sweatless performed the introductions. Wayne sensed the steel of the man when he and Otey shook hands.

'A good piece of work you did, Mr. Wayne,' the promoter said. 'Ellis has been needing to be taken down a peg for quite some time. I've a notion you gave him considerable of a jolt. By the way, if you happen to be around Dallas, drop in and see me; may be to your advantage to do so. Try and make it when you come back from the drive. I expect to have some business to transact in Dodge City shortly. May see you there. No, Sweatless, no more to drink; I'm going to bed.'

With a nod and a smile he took his leave. Wayne regarded his tall form as he crossed to the door.

'I wonder what he has in mind?' he remarked to Sweatless.

'Hard to tell,' replied the saloon-keeper. 'I've a notion you impressed him favourably.'

'By knocking another man down?'

Sweatless shrugged. 'Perhaps. Or perhaps by the way you handled those irons of yours.'

CHAPTER FOUR

The shipping herds rolled north the following morning, Ran Ellis's Boxed E contingent of six hundred cows bringing up the rear and keeping some distance back from the big Forked S bunch.

'Glad to have them there,' commented Lafe Swanson. 'The last herd of a drive is the one that usually catches it if some enterprising gents with share-the-wealth notions make a try.'

Jim Wayne nodded agreement.

The drive to the Red River, ninety miles to the north, was singularly uneventful. In the most beautiful weather the herd grazed along, the hands having little to do. But when they reached the environs of the Red, the fun began. All afternoon the clouds had been banking in the north-west, and when the herds were bedded down at dusk, a half-mile or so south of the river, a mist of rain was falling, a strengthening wind blowing.

Wayne and others had ridden ahead to find the Red already swollen by rains farther north. The Forked S range boss eyed the yellow flood dubiously.

'I think we can make it tomorrow if no more water comes down,' he decided. 'But if it's raining heavily up above here, it's hard to tell. And I've a notion we're liable to catch it here before morning.'

His companions nodded sober agreement. There might be a wild night in store.

Ward Handley, the trail boss, a grizzled veteran of many drives, drew Wayne aside.

'Jim, I don't like the feel of this wind,' he said. 'It's blowing stronger all the time. I've experienced this sort before, and it almost always means bad rain and maybe thunder and lightning, which won't help. The cows are nervous already. And if it gets worse than it is now it'll be a perfect night for the blankety-blank wide-loopers to operate. I'm afraid there won't be any sleep for anybody tonight. Pass the word along for everybody to be up on their toes and on the lookout for trouble. May blow over, but you never can tell, and we can't afford to take chances.'

Wayne was impressed by the warning, for he knew Handley was perfectly familiar with the Red River region and its vagaries. He sought out Ran Ellis, with whom he had become quite friendly in the course of the drive.

'Get your cows up closer,' he told the Boxed E owner. 'Don't let them straggle back. On such a night, there's always the chance of a stampede, and maybe something else.'

Ellis nodded soberly. 'I've got a feeling it's going to be a ripsnorter,' he replied. 'If the cows really get on the prod we're liable to have a mess on our hands we won't forget for quite a while.'

He was right. Just before midnight all hell broke loose. A streak of blue fire split the black sky from zenith to horizon; the accompanying bellow of thunder was like the opening gun of an artillery battle. Flash after flash weaved and zigzagged across the rain-drenched heavens. Lances of flame hissed along the streaming prairie.

During the periods of dazzling radiance, Wayne could see the frightened cattle moving and milling. The cursing cowboys fought to control them to keep the herds from drifting together, but with little success. The perturbed and bewildered cows sought one another's company for protection from the terror loosed in the skies.

'There's no stopping them,' Ran Ellis shouted to Wayne as they met for a moment in the brilliance of a lightning flash, and raced away.

Wayne started on an inspection tour in an endeavour to ascertain how much damage had already been done and what more was to be expected. He was riding on the outskirts of one of the herds when there came a sudden lull in the storm. For a moment the wind almost ceased. And in the unnatural silence there sounded a sharp crackling, as of thorns burning briskly. He strained his ears to listen, but there was no repetition of the sound.

'Feller,' he said to the sorrel, 'that sure sounded like shooting. Now what?'

The wind bellowed again. There was a flash, and in the glare he saw, some distance ahead, a bunch of cows charging across the prairie and several riders who were apparently trying to turn them. He quickened his horse's pace in an attempt to lend a hand as the darkness closed down again.

From the churning jaws of the unholy cloud wrack above burst a torrent of fire, a veritable flame spout that seemed to strike the earth directly in front of him. There was a shattering roar of thunder, and it seemed as if the very sluice gates of heaven were opened to release a liquid wall of icy rain.

Blinded, deafened, all sense of direction

lost, he pulled the sorrel to a halt.

'That was close,' he muttered aloud. 'Guess the boys will have to turn those cows without my help; I've not the slightest notion which way they went. Blazes, what a night!'

However, that last supreme effort of the cantankerous weather gods appeared to climax the storm. The wind began to lose force, and the lightning and the thunder rolled away into the south-east. The rain lessened, became a drizzle, then ceased altogether. The thunder died to a murmur in the far distance. The wind stilled.

Fires were beginning to glimmer where the chuck wagons were stationed. The cooks were getting gallons of steaming coffee ready to revive the nearly exhausted cowboys who, their chore finished for the moment, were drifting in.

Wayne realized that his teeth were chattering with cold. He turned Flame's nose towards the glow of the fires; he badly needed something to take the chill out of his bones.

Arriving at the chuck wagon, he stripped off the rig and gave the sorrel a rub down, then turned it loose to graze. Old Pete had coffee ready for him, and some sandwiches he had managed to manufacture. Wayne drank the coffee, so hot he could hardly swallow it, ate the sandwiches and felt much better.

The hands were appearing, worn out but fairly well satisfied with the night's work.

'It's a mess, but I think we held them all,' Slim Williams told Wayne.

'I saw one bunch skalleyhooting,' the range boss observed. 'However, some of the boys were after them, and I imagine they got them turned.' Williams nodded and drank some more coffee.

Not bothering to break out his bedroll, Wayne curled up with a blanket, using his wet saddle for a pillow, and slept soundly for a couple of hours. When he awakened, the stars were dwindling to pinpoints of steel and there was a streak of rose in the east. He got up, shook himself and drank some more coffee. After a cigarette he felt fit for anything.

Daybreak showed one great herd of nearly twenty thousand cattle. The various bunches were tangled together in a mess that would require days to straighten out.

That was bad enough, but there was worse. For, glazed, unseeing eyes glaring up to greet the dawn, on the soaked prairie a dead man lay.

CHAPTER FIVE

It was Val Rader, the Boxed E range boss, who made the grisly discovery. He rode at top speed to the Forked S camp.

'I'm pretty sure it's one of your boys,' he told Wayne. 'Oh, he's cashed in, all right. I didn't stop to examine him — figured you should do that — but I saw at a glance he was done for. Stampede went over him? I don't think so. Didn't look smashed up. Come on; I'll show you.'

Wayne had already saddled up, and so had Slim Williams, who accompanied them. So little more than ten minutes elapsed before they reached the body.

'Yes, it's one of our boys — Bob Randolph,' Wayne said quietly as they dismounted. 'And he wasn't caught under a stampede.'

Examination showed that Randolph had been shot twice through the chest.

'Never knew what hit him,' Rader mut-

47

tered. 'One slug got him dead centre.'

Jim Wayne stood up and gazed towards the shadowy hills to the south-west, his eyes cold as frosted steel, his face bleak. But when he spoke, his voice was still quiet.

'Remember me mentioning that I saw a bunch of cows hightailing last night, and what I thought was some of our hands trying to turn them?' he remarked to Slim Williams. 'Well, I think we'll be short some stock, too. Those cows I spotted weren't stampeding; they were being run off. I thought I heard shooting just before I saw them. Randolph evidently got in the way and was downed. I was going to try to give a hand to what I thought was some of our boys trying to turn the bunch, but just then that big lightning flash hit the ground nearby and I lost track of them.'

'Darn lucky for you that you did,' growled Rader. 'Otherwise you'd have got it, too.'

'Quite likely,' Wayne admitted. 'I'd have ridden right up to the hellions before I realized what was going on.'

Nearby was Randolph's horse, trying to graze. Wayne got the rig off so the animal could feed in comfort. Then he carefully quartered the ground about the body.

'Here's his gun,' he announced a little later. 'Three empty shells in the chambers. I hope he made every one of those slugs count.'

The word had spread like wildfire, and soon all members of the drive were grouped around the body, cursing bitterly.

'I had a feeling last night, Jim, that something was going to happen,' said Ran Ellis. 'The hyderphobia skunks! What are we going to do about it?'

'There's nothing to do,' Wayne replied wearily. 'They have a big head start, and the rain will have obliterated all signs of their passing. Those cows are headed for New Mexico, the chances are. Well, we'll pack poor Bob to the wagons and give him a decent burial.'

So a little later there was still another low mound on the banks of the Red.

It took six long hard days to get the herds separated and straightened out. Finally all the strays were put where they belonged and the drive was ready to roll again.

'Anyhow, we would have had to wait until now for that blasted river to go down to something like normal,' Lafe Swanson observed philosophically; 'and the boys were better off than being idle all that time. How many do you figure we lost that night, Jim?'

'Would appear my guess was fairly

accurate,' Wayne replied. 'As far as I can estimate, we lost a hundred and ninety-three head.'

'And you still think it wasn't a local bunch from the hills who pulled the wide-looping?'

'Definitely not,' Wayne answered. 'It was handled too expertly not to have been planned in advance. They knew right where to strike and whose cows to tie on to. You know, your stock is far and away the best of the drive. They passed up Ellis's and made the play for our critters, which are much better than his.'

'Yes, we got good cows, thanks to your learning at school how to breed scientifically and improve the stock,' agreed Swanson. 'We'll get top prices. Wonder who in blazes down at Fort Worth was keeping an eye on us?'

'A question I'd very much like to have the answer to,' Wayne replied grimly. 'Maybe I'll get it; I sure hope so.'

The Red was crossed without untoward incident or loss of stock, and the drive rolled northward along a well-defined trail several hundred yards wide. During the course of the years a million pounding hoofs had churned the ground to dust which the wind blew away, so that the trail was in the nature of a shallow ditch, its surface lower than the adjoining prairie. The white skulls and bleached skeletons of longhorns were to be seen, and here and there a low mound, grass-grown, such as marked the last resting-place of young Bob Randolph, the Forked S puncher.

Ward Handley, the trail boss, dropped back for a chat with Wayne.

'Jim, you sure called the turn there at the Red,' he observed. 'Things worked out just as you predicted they would. You had the low-down better'n I did, and I've made this drive a dozen times. Why, way down at Fort Worth you predicted we'd hit bad weather at the Red and that the Red would be in flood. How'd you do it?'

'It's just that I've made a study of climatic conditions up here and to the north-west,' Wayne replied. 'I learned all I could about the prevailing winds and their meaning, and the meaning of a sudden shift of the wind, and the spacing of storms, which I found was fairly even. At Fort Worth I learned when the last hard storm hit up here and figured another was due about the time we'd hit the Red. Of course I could have been wide of the mark, for weather is erratic, to put it mildly.'

'But you weren't,' said Handley. 'Guess

educated young fellers figure things better even than us old-timers with a heap of experience.'

'Something for you to keep in mind, Ward, for future reference,' Wayne added. 'The country around Fort Worth is and always will be less plagued by bad blizzards such as they have over to the west and north. Which means something where stock raising is concerned.'

The old trail boss shot him a curious glance.

'Sorta interested in Forth Worth, ain't you, Jim?'

'Yes, I am,' Wayne admitted. 'And speaking of predictions, I'll venture another: I predict that eventually Fort Worth will be the concentration centre for the livestock industry of the South-west, that it will have the largest stockyards south of St. Louis. Remember what I tell you.'

Handley nodded, then remarked, 'Folks are saying the railroad won't ever get there.'

'They said the same thing about the Union Pacific, but it did,' Wayne retorted. 'The railroad will get to Fort Worth. Of that I'm confident, confident enough to gamble on it.'

'Could be,' Handley conceded. He grinned. 'I'm getting a mite old to be maverickin' around, but I do still get itchy feet now and then. You and me'll have another little talk later on.'

'Agreed,' said Wayne, smiling broadly. He figured he had just about 'hired' a highly efficient range boss.

Handley gazed ahead. 'Next crossing, aside from a creek or two, is the Cimarron,' he observed. 'And the Cimarron is always bad, full of quicksands that'll bog down a steer or a horse in no time. I've seen the water come down all of a sudden in solid sheets. It stirs up the sand from the bottom, and trying to swim it is like trying to swim through mud — you just can't do it. And it'll happen so darn sudden that a herd can be caught and darn near every critter drowned. You can't take chances with the Cimarron, or the Salt Fork of the Arkansas, when flood water's coming down. Other times, though, the Cimarron is just a sandy stretch with not much current. Maybe we'll be lucky.'

They did get a break at the Cimarron. The river was low, the crossing negotiated without difficulty. It was nearing noon when the last beef sloshed through the mud and water, but the drive kept right on moving by orders of the trail boss, whose word was absolute law on a drive.

'Well, guess I'd better be getting up front,' Handley said. 'I'll try and call a halt so that everybody will have a decent bedding ground without getting the herds too close together; don't want such another mixup as we had at the Red. When you see the dust begin to settle up front, pick out what you figure to be a good spot.'

'Okay,' Wayne replied. 'Take care of yourself.'

Chapter Six

Wayne had covered some five miles when he saw a gleam of water ahead. It turned out to be a small stream running from the mouth of a narrow and brush-grown canyon and cutting straight across the trail. He glanced to the north; the swarthy dust cloud raised by the moving cattle was no longer visible. Evidently the other herds had found suitable spots for bedding down.

'We're quite a way behind the next bunch, but I figure this should be it,' he told old Pete, the cook. 'We'll squat on the west side of the trail; Ellis can take the east. That'll keep the herds separated enough. I don't think it's a good notion for us to move on from here. Soon be dark. Yes, this will do.'

Old Pete got busy with his pots and pans and Dutch ovens.

Supper around the campfire was an hilarious affair, for the drive was drawing to a close; Dodge City and its pleasures were not too far off. Everybody was happy and carefree; that is, everybody but Jim Wayne. He was very well satisfied with the bedding ground except for one thing — a dark and ominous canyon mouth which yawned about an eighth of a mile south of the camp.

He told himself he was being foolish, that there was scant danger of an untoward happening so close to the Cimarron crossing. If anything was in the making, it would more likely be attempted in the more broken country south of the Arkansas. But the premonition persisted, grew stronger as the hands settled down to rest, leaving only the lonely night hawks riding slowly around the herd.

Wayne lay down and tried to sleep. The relief men of the second guard period came on duty. An hour passed, another, and he could not sleep. The black mouth of that canyon was continually before his eyes.

An hour or so before midnight he gave up. Cursing his no doubt senseless apprehension, he secured his Winchester, slipped silently from the camp and headed for the vicinity of the canyon mouth on foot; he could hardly hope to get the rig on Flame without arousing somebody.

Close to the canyon mouth and less than a hundred yards to the north of its north wall was a straggle of thicket. He holed up in the growth, making himself as comfortable as circumstances and conditions allowed. The sky was slightly overcast, but the clouds were thinning, breaking up, with the promise of brilliant starlight to come.

The clouds thinned more and more. Soon he could see for some distance across the prairie. A little later the cattle became clearly visible, and the figure of the night hawk slowly pacing his horse around the south end of the herd. And as the light grew, nearby objects took on definite form and shape. Nothing could come out of that blasted canyon that he couldn't view in detail.

But the canyon mouth remained dark and silent. No sound came from its depths. There was no sign of movement amid the brush. Wayne began to feel a bit silly.

And then, when the time approached for the 'graveyard shift' to take over the riding chore, he heard something that tensed every sense to hair-trigger alertness — the faint but unmistakable jingling of a bridle iron. And the sound came from the canyon.

Nerves strained to the breaking-point, he stared at the dark opening. Again that musical tinkle. Then more solid shadows loomed amid the shadows of the gorge mouth.

Another moment and nearly a dozen horse-men rode from the canyon. They rode slowly, purposefully, towards the bedded herd.

Wayne half raised the rifle, then hesitated; Jim Wayne had never shot to kill. And he could be mistaken. The riders might be only harmless cowhands returning from some chore. But why that stealthy, purposeful ap-proach?

Abruptly the group halted. The night hawk had appeared around the edge of the herd, riding slowly, his attention directed towards the cows. Wayne saw the leading horseman raise a rifle and take deliberate aim.

Wayne knew he'd have to act quickly to save the night hawk's life. He clamped the Winchester to his shoulder; his pale eyes glanced along the sights.

The long gun bucked. Fire spurted from its muzzle. The report rang out like thunder in the stillness of the night. The mounted rifleman whirled sideways in his saddle and pitched to the ground.

A chorus of startled yells arose, then a bel-low of gunfire. Bullets whipped the growth, showering Wayne with leaves and twigs, fan-ning his face with their lethal breath. He shifted the Winchester muzzle a trifle and squeezed the trigger.

A second man slumped forward and slid from the hull. Answering slugs stormed about Wayne. One ripped through the sleeve of his shirt, sliced the flesh of his arm and nearly hurled him off his feet with shock. He steadied himself and fired as fast as he could pull trigger.

A third raider went down. Yet another reeled but grabbed the saddle-horn and stayed in the hull.

That was enough for the wide-loopers. Howling curses, and firing wildly at the dark growth, they whirled their horses and streaked back to the canyon mouth, one lurching and swaying and clinging to the horn for support. Wayne, his rifle empty, flopped to the ground as bullets loosed at random still came uncomfortably close. Another moment and the mouth of the gorge had swallowed the band of night riders. No more shots came from the shadowy depths.

From the Forked S camp came shouts. Wayne drew one of his Colts and fired three evenly spaced shots in the air — the rangeland's call for help. Then he arose, reloaded his rifle and cautiously approached the three forms sprawled on the ground, gun ready for instant action. For he knew a wounded outlaw could be as dangerous as a broken-backed rattler.

However, there came no sound or movement from the unsavoury trio. Evidently he had drilled them dead centre. He paused, suddenly experiencing a sickish feeling in the pit of his stomach. A film of perspiration formed on his upper lip and the palms of his hands. Jim Wayne had never before killed a man, and it was not pleasant to look upon his handiwork.

At that moment a shot sounded from the night hawk, who was discreetly staying right where he was.

'Over this way,' Wayne called as he recognized the voice. 'Over this way, Craig — it's Wayne.'

The night hawk approached cautiously until he was sure it was really the range boss talking; then he quickened his horse's pace and soon was beside Wayne. From the north came a thunder of hoofs as the Forked S hands raced at top speed in answer to Wayne's signal. A moment later they jerked their foaming horses to a halt, volleying questions.

Wayne explained briefly, for suddenly he was feeling very tired. Profanity crackled. Craig Hoyt, the night hawk, raised a hand and mopped his face, although the night was cool.

'Much obliged, Jim,' he said thickly. 'I won't forget it.'

From the direction of the herd came a pounding of hoofs. The cowboys who had dismounted and grouped around the bodies whirled, hands streaking to their guns.

'It's Ran Ellis and his bunch,' Wayne said a moment later. 'Guess they heard the shooting and are coming to see what's up.'

The Boxed E rannies arrived and their questions answered, old Lafe Swanson took over the talking, for which Wayne was thankful.

'Jim, how the devil did you catch on?' he asked Wayne.

'I just played a hunch,' the range boss replied. 'I couldn't shake off a presentiment that something was going to happen, so I came down here where I could keep an eye on that infernal crack in the hills.'

'And darned lucky for me,' said Craig Hoyt.

'Yes, the sidewinders would have killed you, cut out a few hundred head and been back in the canyon before we tumbled to what was going on,' growled Swanson. 'A good chore, Jim; a mighty good chore. *I* won't forget it, either.'

Ran Ellis spoke up. 'I think it would be a

good notion to pack those carcasses to the campfire and give them a careful once-over; might learn something worth while.'

Wayne nodded. 'I've a notion you're right,' he said. 'Go ahead, some of you. I'd rather not touch them just yet.'

'Reckon I can understand how you feel,' Ellis remarked sympathetically. 'Been through it myself; not three at a time, though. Had trouble sleeping well for a while.'

Jim Wayne's lips tightened.

The bodies were draped across saddles. The three riders led the horses they had volunteered for the chore, Wayne walking beside them, the others bringing up the rear.

Old Pete, cursing everything and everybody for disturbing his rest, had coffee on the boil when they arrived at the camp.

The bodies were laid out where the glow of the fire would play on them. Val Rader, the Boxed E range boss, suddenly uttered an exclamation.

'I'll swear I saw this chunky one down at Fort Worth,' he declared. 'I remember that crooked nose.'

'Just as I said after what happened during the storm down on the Red,' Wayne remarked. 'We've been trailed ever since we left Fort Worth. It's an organized bunch.'

'Well, these three are sort of *dis*-organized,' Swanson commented dryly. 'I'm going through their pockets — might turn up something of interest.

'Packing a hefty passel of dinero,' he added as he heaped coin and bills on the grass. 'The devils have been doing all right by themselves. What shall we do with the money, Jim? They're your game and you have the say.'

'Divide it among the boys,' Wayne replied. 'I don't want any of it.'

However, nobody else was squeamish about accepting the unexpected windfall, which would go to swell the coffers of Dodge City saloon-keepers.

'Nothing else to amount to anything,' Swanson said after the chore was finished. 'Regulation irons they're packing. You say the horses followed the others into the canyon, Jim? A pity they didn't stay behind. Brands might have told us something.'

'Not likely,' said Wayne. 'That sort usually fork Mexican skillet-of-snake burns that mean nothing, or unregistered brands that can't be traced to any outfit.'

'Expect you're right,' conceded Swanson. 'Well, I reckon we'd better try and get a little more sleep. And I think tomorrow we should not lag too far behind the other outfits. If tonight is a fair sample, no telling what else might be in store for us before we reach the Arkansas.'

CHAPTER SEVEN

Despite his fears to the contrary, Wayne slept soundly for several hours and awoke feeling much better.

The drive rolled on. Mindful of Swanson's suggestion, Wayne pushed the cows until they were only a reasonable distance behind the Walking R. Old Lafe might have the right notion. Better to risk tangling with another herd than to lay themselves open to something similar to the happening of the night before.

A rider had been sent ahead to acquaint the other owners with the attempted wide-looping and to warn them to be on their guard.

That night both the Forked S and the Boxed E bedded down on open prairie, where nobody could approach without being spotted a long way off. The night passed without incident and the drive rolled on in the early morning.

'I've a feeling we won't have any more trouble between here and Dodge City,' old Lafe predicted. 'I figure, Jim, that you gave the hellions a bellyful they won't forget for a while.'

Whatever the reason, Swanson was right. Nothing happened; and with a sigh of relief, Handley, the drive boss, saw the flood of the Arkansas River winding and shining in the sun. The crossing was negotiated without difficulty, and the tallying and weighing in began, the chore being finished before dark.

The Nueces cowboys, their chore finished, were paid off and headed for town. The Forked S bunch and Ellis's Boxed E hands chose the Trail's End Saloon, a big, boisterous and fairly well lighted place, for their first stop.

'And I hope it won't be the last one for some of them,' grumbled old Lafe. 'Our boys ain't so bad, but I get the jumps when I look at those Boxed E hellions. They're a salty bunch, and Ellis himself and his dratted range boss are the worst of the lot. Keep an eye on our punchers, Jim, and try and keep them out of trouble.'

Wayne promised to do so to the best of his ability. He agreed with Swanson that Ran Ellis and his riders were salty, but he did not think they would deliberately go looking for trouble. No telling what might happen, though, once red-eye got to buzzing in their ears. He believed he could pretty well control his own men, and Ellis seemed to defer to him. As one of the Boxed E hands said, 'Ran loves a man who can lick him, and he ain't had to love many, I reckon. He'll follow your lead anywhere, Wayne, and for all his temper, he's a good man to have at your back if a ruckus cuts loose.'

To which Jim Wayne was ready to agree.

Things were lively at the Trail's End, although the real rush had not yet begun. The cowboys lined up at the bar and ordered drinks.

The Trail's End was located on the northern edge of Hell's Half Acre, which lay between the Santa Fé Railroad tracks and the Arkansas River. It was not much frequented by gentlemen of means and unblemished reputations, so Wayne was more than a little surprised when a tall, handsome, tawny-haired, impeccably dressed man entered and made his way to the bar. It was Malcolm Otey, the Dallas real estate dealer.

Otey spotted Wayne and moved down the bar until he was beside him. He held out his slender, manicured hand.

'How are you, Mr. Wayne?' he said. 'Told you I might be up this way when you arrived. Have a good trip?'

'Turned out fairly well,' Wayne conceded.

'Glad to hear it,' said Otey. 'I'm staying at the Dodge House, Deacon Cox's hotel on Front Street, two blocks east of Second Avenue. If you have a chance, drop in and see me tomorrow afternoon. I'll be in the lobby around two o'clock. I'd like to have a talk with you. Right now we'll have a drink.'

'How'd you know I was here?' Wayne asked as he accepted the invitation.

'Didn't know it,' replied Otey, smiling his thin smile. 'Just figured this was likely to be first stop for the drive hands. If I hadn't found you here, I'd have looked farther south. Felt pretty sure you'd accompany your men.'

'Sort of woolly down there,' Wayne commented. Otey shrugged his broad shoulders.

'Any place in Dodge City is woolly, under certain conditions and circumstances,' he countered.

Otey tossed off his glass, and with a smile and a nod left the saloon. Wayne gazed at his tall and graceful form as he passed through the swinging doors.

'That gent 'pears to have taken a fancy to

68

you, Jim,' Ran Ellis, who had overheard the conversation, remarked. 'I heard a thing or two about him in Fort Worth. Seems he's up and coming in Dallas. Has some interests in Fort Worth, too, I'd say from what I heard.'

'Very likely,' Wayne conceded. 'Wonder what he wants to see me about? In Fort Worth he asked me to drop in on him at Dallas if I could find time to ride over that way when we came back from the drive.'

'Reckon he'll tell you if you visit him at the hotel tomorrow like he asked you to,' Ellis said.

Wayne was mildly curious as to what proposition Otey had in mind; whatever it was, he was not interested. He had determined to acquire a spread in the vicinity of Fort Worth and would allow nothing to deflect him.

The Trail's End was filling up and growing more boisterous by the minute. An orchestra was playing and there were dancers on the floor. The bar was crowded, the tables becoming occupied. Wayne felt his pulses quicken as he surveyed the animated and colourful scene. After all, he was young, and after the grim happenings on the drive he was glad of a chance to relax a little and let himself go.

Ellis appeared to be likewise affected, for his eyes sparkled and he chattered gaily. Even the saturnine Val Rader seemed to be getting into the spirit of things. He grinned and bobbed and traded quips with those near him. All in all, it was a welcome spree in town.

Wayne noticed that, as appeared to be habitual with him, Ellis's hot blue eyes were never still. They were constantly roving about the room, centring on the swinging doors, studying open windows.

'Looking for somebody, Ran?' he asked casually. Ellis shrugged his big shoulders.

'I'm always looking for *somebody*,' he countered. 'As you may have heard, I have a sort of a reputation down in Fort Worth — there are folks who look sideways at me. Guess I earned it. I never stole anything, but for a while in certain sections my gun was for hire — that's how I got the stake to buy my spread. No secret that big owners sometimes hire fast gunhands to protect their property, and sometimes it's a good deal of a chore. Was in my case. I pulled trigger quite a few times. That's why I said that I knew how you felt when you downed those three hellions by the Cimarron. Felt that way myself the first time I downed a jigger. You get over that after a bit, though, and the next one don't come so hard.'

'Something I'm a bit afraid of,' Wayne interpolated. 'And I have no desire to become a killer.' Ellis nodded.

'Funny things are forced on a feller now and then, though,' he observed. 'Happened that way with me. After the first one I was forced to shoot again, and several times more. And, incidentally, a hired gun makes enemies. That's why I'm always sort of on the lookout. You'll notice Val Rader is a good deal the same way; he was with me in those days when we worked for the McLane outfit.'

Wayne nodded soberly. He had heard of the war the McLane outfit waged against rivals, and it was a grim story.

Ellis was silent for a few moments; then he said impressively, 'But I'm not looking out for myself tonight; I'm looking out for you.'

Wayne stared. 'For me?'

'That's right. When you downed those three skunks you made enemies, and don't forget it. The rest of the bunch will be out to even the score. And it won't be just a hankering for revenge, the chances are. They'll look upon you as dangerous, something that must be gotten out of the way. You not only outshot them; you also outsmarted them. That, they'll figure, makes you doubly dangerous. A hired gun rides mighty close to outlaw land, Jim, and learns to think as owlhoots think. You've never had that experience. Tonight you've paid very little attention to anybody here or to folks coming in and going out. I'm very much afraid that you'll change your attitude if you manage to stay alive; that's one of the penalties you pay for a killing. And because I know how the outlaw mind works, I've been keeping a close watch on things tonight. Right now somebody may be looking for you, and not with an opera glass. Understand what I mean?'

'I'm afraid I do,' Wayne said slowly. 'Thanks for the tip, and thanks for looking out for me as you've been doing; I'll try and use better judgment from now on.

'I heard some yarns told about you,' he admitted. 'One of them made me laugh.'

'What one was that?' Ellis asked.

'The one that said coloured people maintained you are Cullen Barnet come back to life,' Wayne replied with a smile.

Ellis didn't laugh and he didn't smile. He shot Wayne a peculiar look.

'I'm not Cullen Barnet and never was,' he said. 'I've a notion some coloured folks started that yarn because I'm big and tall, like Barnet, and because my place is close to the Big Hickory Bottoms and I ride around the edge of the Bottoms now and then — the section interests me. But they're not joking when they say old Cullen has come back to life; they're dead in earnest. They really believe he's back operating from the Bottoms. He was a strange character, all right, judging from what I've been able to learn of him. Folks who claim to know say he was an educated man who had once been a gentleman, and that although he worked out of the Bottoms, he had connections in Mexico and elsewhere and smuggled stuff all the way to San Antonio and Dallas. And they say that nobody ever got a really good look at Cullen Barnet's face, that he always had a big hat with a wide brim pulled down over his eyes and a neckerchief up around his mouth. Of course you can take all such yarns with a hefty helping of salt, but there's no doubt but that he was an unusual character. The Rangers say they chased somebody they felt was Cullen into the Bottoms and shot him, but they admit they are not sure. They're not even sure that they killed him. They can only say that the man they shot went into the Black Water, and that nobody ever came out of the Black Water alive. I've seen the Black Water and I'll

73

admit it's hard to believe a wounded man could have swum it and got out alive.

'And another thing that was said about him is interesting, and rather unusual for cattleland. It was said there wasn't a safe in the country he couldn't bust open.'

'Somewhat of an exaggeration, I'd say,' Wayne replied. 'But most of the safes in cow country are not much more than old iron boxes with a handle and a simple combination knob on the door, so a real cracksman wouldn't have much difficulty opening them. Not many of that kind of gentry show up on the range, although I've heard of a few.'

Ellis nodded. 'It's said Cullen hated coloured folks and killed quite a few of them wantonly. One thing's sure for certain: the coloured folks who farm their little patches around the edge of the Bottoms are scared.

'So,' he added smilingly, 'if you take a notion to come back to the Fort Worth section, look out for Cullen Barnet.'

Then, more seriously, 'Meanwhile keep your eyes open for something a heap worse than a resurrected Cullen Barnet — the hellions you tangled with down by the Cimarron.'

Wayne nodded soberly, for he was inclined to take Ellis's warning at face value; it was certainly not illogical. No doubt the outlaw bunch was considerably riled over the frustration of their wide-looping attempt and the killing of three of their number. Very likely they *would* be out to even up the score.

Ellis tossed off his drink and searched the room again with his eyes.

'Everything looks okay,' he remarked. 'I'm getting restless. Think I'll go out and wander around for a while. Don't forget what I told you, Jim.' He sauntered over to where Val Rader was standing and said a few words. Rader nodded. Ellis waved to Wayne and took his leave.

Eventually Wayne began to grow restless himself. He'd had all that he wanted to drink for the present. A change of scene and a stroll in the cool night air wouldn't be bad. He glanced around, saw that several of the Forked S hands were on the dance floor. A couple more had joined the poker games. The others were grouped at the bar with some of the Boxed E riders. Everything appeared to be under control, but he wouldn't stay away long. He placed his empty glass on the bar and walked out.

Mindful of Ellis's warning, he walked warily, constantly scanning his surroundings as he worked south towards the river. But he was new to this sort of thing and failed to notice the figure slouching along quite a way to the rear, hugging building walls, avoiding patches of light, always keeping him in sight.

CHAPTER EIGHT

It was a beautiful night of bonfire stars, cool and still. Wayne was thoroughly enjoying his stroll.

Soon he could smell the river and decided it was time to retrace his steps; he didn't want to stay away from his hands too long. He turned and trudged back the way he had come.

It was Ran Ellis's warning that saved him. Otherwise Wayne might not have noticed the tight group of shadowy figures lounging in an alley mouth directly ahead. As it was, he halted the instant he sighted them, hands dropping to his holsters. He was ready for action when the group, a half-dozen in number, surged from the alley and fanned out across the street.

Right in front of him was one of the big whisky barrels filled with water that were placed along the streets at convenient intervals to use in case of fire. A single bound and he was crouched behind it.

From up the street came a curse, then the boom of a shot. The slug plunked into the barrel. So, instantly, did several more. Wayne caught sight of a figure running towards the middle of the street and fired twice. The man plunged forward on his face and lay still. Yells of anger rose, and a bellow of gunfire. But a whisky barrel full of water provides excellent shelter, and Wayne still was untouched.

Just the same, he knew he was in a tight spot. The odds were too great; the attackers were fanning out cautiously, and soon he would be surrounded. He risked a quick glance around the bulge of the barrel and emptied one gun at the advancing drygulchers. A scream of agony rent the air, followed by more curses and more shots.

Suddenly Wayne realized that another gun had joined in, farther up the street. The curses changed to yelps of consternation, yells of pain. Help had arrived from some unexpected quarter. Wayne surged erect, his cocked gun ready for action.

The attackers were fleeing wildly back into the alley. Wayne sped them on their way with the last cartridges in the cylinder of his Colt. He was reloading with frantic speed when a running form loomed in a patch of light up the street. He recognized Val Rader.

'You all right, Jim?' Rader shouted anxiously. 'Come on; let's get out of here.'

Men were peering from the door of a poorly lighted saloon across the way, but nobody ventured out as they raced up the street, Rader leading. He whisked around a corner, Wayne panting at his heels, dived into a dark alley, reached another and better lighted street, rounded still another corner and slowed down.

'Guess this oughta do it,' he gasped. 'Figured we'd better hightail. Might be some more of the sons of skunks hanging around down there. Yes, we're okay now. There's Front Street right ahead.'

'How the devil did you come to happen along at just the right time?' Wayne asked.

'Ran told me to keep an eye on you if you went out,' Rader replied. 'I've had you in sight ever since you left the Trail's End. Dropped back a mite too far — didn't want you to spot me — and had to hump myself to get in on the ball.'

'Well, I owe you and Ellis both a lot of thanks,' Wayne said. 'You saved my bacon all right. I figured my number was up.'

Rader's thin lips writhed in what he used for a smile. 'You were doing okay,' he said.

'You downed two of the snakes. They never moved after they hit the ground. I figure I only got one. Maybe nicked a couple more.'

Jim Wayne breathed deeply.

They found the Trail's End going strong but with no indication of trouble. Rader glanced around.

'There's a little table over by the corner of the dance floor that nobody 'pears to be using,' he remarked. 'What say we sit down? My legs feel a mite rubbery after that gallop up from the river.'

'A good notion,' Wayne agreed. 'I can stand taking a load off my feet myself; it was quite a run.'

They were discussing a drink together when, a little later, Ran Ellis strolled in. He glanced about and came over to the table. Drawing up a vacant chair, he favoured them with a searching look.

'Heard there was quite a shooting down on Lee Street, close to the river,' he observed casually, after giving a waiter his order.

'Reckon there was,' Rader agreed.

'All right; let's have it,' said Ellis. 'Figured you two were mixed up in that corpse and cartridge session.'

Rader told him in detail. Ellis nodded his

head sagely.

'Thought something like that might be pulled. Reckon they were on the lookout for you and spotted you when you left here,' he said to Wayne. 'Arranged a nice little lead pizening party for you. How many did you get this time, Jim?'

'He got two,' Rader told him before Wayne could reply. 'When he plugs 'em he plugs 'em dead centre; no fooling.'

'Want to thank you, Ran, for having Val look after me,' Wayne said. 'If it hadn't been for him I figure it would have been curtains for me.'

'Could have been,' conceded Ellis. 'But you're learning fast. Ducking behind that water barrel meant quick thinking. And quick thinking is even better 'n quick pulling. Feller who can do it usually comes out on top. How you feel?'

'Too good, everything considered,' Wayne growled morosely. 'Seems I ought to feel different.'

'You won't,' Ellis declared decisively. 'From now on it'll come easy. Remember what I told you a while ago?'

'Yes, I remember, and I'm afraid you're right,' Wayne answered.

The owners, Swanson, Hubbard and Carter, appeared, and another table was moved into position.

'Not such a bad night, I'd say,' observed Carter as he ordered drinks. 'Nothing really bad so far, I gather. I think the boys will all be in shape to travel tomorrow afternoon. We'll let 'em have another bust in Fort Worth. The quicker we get them away from this place the better I'll feel.' The others nodded agreement.

'Heard some shooting a while back, but I reckon it was just some loose-cinch gents plugging holes in the sky.'

Ellis winked at Wayne. Both kept silent.

After a while, Swanson said, 'Well, looks like things are pretty well under control. I'm going to bed. I'm sleeping at the Dodge House, and I reserved a room for you, Jim.'

'Hubbard and me aim to stay at the Alamo,' remarked Carter. 'Shall we amble?'

The others were agreeable, and they left the saloon. Thoroughly weary from the long hard day and the excitement, Wayne was asleep almost before his head hit the pillow. He slept soundly until mid-morning. After cleaning up a bit, he descended to the lobby, wondering if he would find Malcolm Otey there, for he remembered that he had a tentative appointment with the real estate man for two o'clock.

However, when he mentioned Otey's

name to the desk clerk, he got a surprise.

'Mr. Otey checked out early this morning,' the clerk replied. 'Said he had to get back to Dallas. Seemed sorta put out about something; was real grumpy.'

Wayne visited the stable where Flame was domiciled to make sure everything was okay with the big sorrel. Everything was, and he repaired to the Trail's End for some breakfast. While he was eating, Val Rader came in, looking as if he'd had a busy night.

Evidently he had, for he settled for black coffee and a slice of dry toast and seemed to have difficulty getting that down.

'Ran will be here at any minute,' he said. 'Stopped at the general store for something.'

Ellis arrived a few minutes later and appeared quite chipper.

'Something to going to bed before you get completely ossified,' he said as he ordered a bountiful meal. 'If you fellows are ready, I'm all set to ride as soon as I choke down this surrounding.'

Less than an hour later, they clattered across the bridge to where the wagons were assembled. The hands drifted in, none much the worse for wear, although a few skinned heads and discoloured eyes served as mementos of a hilarious evening.

But their faces were ashine with pleasant

memories and they hurled quips at one another in salty language.

'Met the town marshal this morning,' observed Craig Hoyt, the rider Wayne had saved from getting his come-uppance down by the Cimarron. 'He 'peared out of sorts. Said he got a tip he'd better hustle down to Lee Street, towards the river. When he got there, he found three carcasses. Said he'd be willing to swear they were Texans, and if they were, they were the only good Texans he'd ever clapped eyes on. He don't seem to like us.'

The account was greeted with loud guffaws. 'Told you I only got one,' Val Rader whispered to Wayne. 'I must be slippin'.'

By two o'clock everybody was present and accounted for, and the long trek to the Nueces country began.

The Red was on good behaviour for a change, and the crossing of that unpredictable river was negotiated with no difficulty. In the blue and gold of a fall evening the wagons made camp on the outskirts of Fort Worth and the cowboys sallied forth in search of diversion.

During the weeks of their absence, the town had deteriorated greatly. Everywhere were boarded-up shops and empty windows. Half the saloons had closed, and most of those that remained were doing a very slack business.

Sweatless Sam's Western Star was an exception. When he entered, it seemed to Jim Wayne that the place was as lively and crowded as on the occasion of his previous visit.

Sweatless greeted him warmly and led the way to an isolated table where they could talk undisturbed.

'Yep, I'm doing all right,' Sweatless replied to Wayne's comment.

'And now I've got something to tell you. I've got a good thing lined up for you, with only one drawback, as far as I can see. A nice little spread that the owner, a feller named Jess Higginbottom, is plumb anxious to let go in a hurry. 'Pears to have something lined up over east. It's a good holding, well grassed, with plenty of water. Some cows he'll throw in — he got rid of most of his stock a while back.'

'And the price?' Wayne asked. Sweatless named it. Wayne considered for a moment.

'I can swing that,' he said. 'And I figure I can get the cows I need from Uncle Lafe Swanson, on terms. What's the drawback you mentioned?'

Sweatless glanced around and lowered his voice.

'Your neighbour on the south-east is Ran Ellis.'

Wayne laughed. 'I've a notion I could do worse,' he said. 'I don't consider that a drawback I need to give much thought to.'

'Okay,' Sweatless conceded dubiously, 'but if he don't get you into a ruckus of some kind sooner or later, I miss my guess.'

'I'll chance it.' Wayne smiled. 'When can I get in touch with your man Higginbottom?'

'Tomorrow afternoon I'll ride with you to see him,' replied Sweatless. 'Just a couple of hours to his *casa* which, incidentally, is a good ranch-house. Other buildings are okay, too, and in pretty good repair.'

'Sounds better all the time,' Wayne said. 'Thanks a lot, Sam, for all you've done for me; I certainly appreciate it.'

'I'm serving my own interests,' Sweatless replied. 'We need up-and-coming young fellers like you to get this town going again. You and the young hellions you bring in will hand me plenty of business. Well, guess I'd better circulate a mite and see how the boys are making out.'

Lafe Swanson came in a few minutes later and occupied the chair Sweatless vacated. Wayne at once informed him of his decision and detailed what Sweatless had told him. Swanson nodded his wise old head.

'Sounds good, if you really believe this section is going to pick up,' he said. 'Price is reasonable, I'd say, if everything is as Sweatless says. Okay; I've got more than that in cash in the wagon. I'll advance you the amount so you can close the deal pronto, if you're satisfied after looking over the holding. You can give me a cheque for it when we get back to the Nueces; be glad to get the darned stuff off my hands. And I'll let you have what cows you need to get going. Pay for 'em when you're able.'

He waved away Wayne's thanks. 'I want to see you get ahead, Jim,' he said. 'You're a top hand, but there's no sense in you working all your life for somebody else. With what your dad left you and what you've saved, you're in a position to strike out on your own. I've a notion you'll make a go of it. If you don't, you're young and have plenty of time to start over again some place else. Let's have a drink.'

Wayne left the saloon early, for he was too full of plans for the future to take much interest in drinking and celebration. He wanted to be alone where he could think.

At two o'clock the following afternoon, he and Sweatless set out to visit the owner of the JH. Wayne was impressed by the excellence of the range they crossed and said so.

'Figured you'd cotton to it,' replied Sweatless. 'Oh, I know a good holding when I see one, even if it ain't got glass around it.'

Jess Higginbottom proved to be a benign old-timer with a snowy beard.

'Was plumb pleased when Sweatless told me about you hankering to buy a spread hereabouts,' he said. 'I've been wanting to sell out and head over to Louisiana where my son is doing well by himself. He's been asking me to come and live with him for quite a spell, and I figured that with things going to pot hereabouts, now would be a good time to do it, if I could manage to unload this turkey on to some loco gent.'

'I've a feeling, Mr. Higginbottom, that it is not going to prove a turkey,' Wayne differed with a smile.

'You could be right,' the old gentleman conceded. 'Anyhow, it's good for young fellows to start at the bottom and fight their way to the top. I'll write you out a bill of sale, and after we've had a snack we'll ride to town and have it notarized and put in proper legal shape. I understand that young lawyer feller Matt Jarret is still in Fort Worth and 'lows to stay. *He* says, too, that Fort Worth is going to come out top dog before the last brand's run. He'll take care of everything for us.'

As a result of the decision, before the first stars blossomed in the sky Jim Wayne was the owner of the JH.

CHAPTER NINE

Wayne decided to keep the registered JH brand. 'As good as any and no easier to change than most,' he said to Swanson. 'Not much sense in trying to devise a burn that can't be altered. A really clever "rewrite" man can change any combination into something else.'

'The idea is to keep a jump ahead of brand blotters and like gents,' agreed Swanson. 'A good dose of lead pizenin' or the noosed end of a rope will usually do the trick. Well, we'll head for the Nueces tomorrow, and then you can amble back this way with your cows and be all ready to set yourself up in business. I imagine you won't have any trouble hiring some hands down our way; plenty of young fellers who'll like to trail their twine for a spell.'

Wayne at once got in touch with Ward Handley, acquainted him with what he had done and offered him a job as range boss of the JH. Handley chuckled and grinned.

'Felt pretty sure you had just that in mind when we talked about Fort Worth a while back,' he said. 'Told you then I was getting a case of itchy feet — remember? Well, they're rarin' to go places, and I reckon you've done hired yourself a hand.'

They had a drink together to seal the bargain.

'And I know a few fellers who'll be glad to sign up with you, too,' Handley added.

'That'll help,' Wayne replied. 'Anybody you pick is okay with me. I aim to pay a little better than the average scale. I figure it's a good way to come out ahead in the end.'

'It is,' Handley agreed. 'A free-handed boss gets more work out of his riders than a stingy one, and holds his hands. Okay; much obliged, Jim.'

'And thank you for coming along with me on what is to a certain extent a gamble,' Wayne replied.

'I like to gamble,' Handley declared cheerfully, and ambled off to make sure everything was all set for the long ride back to the Nueces.

Old Ward, Wayne reflected, was in the nature of being an object lesson. He was a top hand and he knew every angle of the cattle business, but at his age he was still working for wages. Maybe that could be changed. He determined, if he made a go of his undertaking, to try to induce Handley to invest a portion of his wages in the spread each month. Then when the last roundup drew near, the old man would have his loop tight on something solid.

Wayne next got in touch with Ran Ellis. The Boxed E owner was enthusiastic.

'You've got the plumb right notion, Jim,' he said. 'This is going to be an up-and-coming section before you know it.

'Those horned toads who are leaving' — he added contemptuously — 'their guts have turned to fiddle strings. You could take a bunch of corncobs and lightning bugs and make them run till their tongues hang out like calf ropes! Good riddance; we don't want that sort here. This is a country for men. As soon as old Higginbottom pulls out, which I reckon he'll do pronto, I'm going to send two or three of my boys to coil their twine in your *casa* and keep an eye on things till you get back.'

'That's mighty fine of you, Ran,' Wayne accepted gratefully. 'I was wondering if I couldn't hire somebody to handle that chore for me.'

'Don't go bothering about any hiring,' Ellis replied. 'And don't thank me. You see, I ain't forgot that you cottoned to me when a lot of folks, including some on the drive, were sorta looking sideways at me. You changed their notions for them, and don't I know it! And I'm not forgetting. Okay; so long. Be seeing you soon. You say you hired Handley for your range boss? Fine! You couldn't have tied on to a better hand.'

So, everything considered, Jim Wayne headed back for the Nueces in a highly satisfied state of mind. Things were working out even better than he had hoped for.

It was a long drive and a hard drive from the Nueces River to Fort Worth on the Trinity. But with each advancing mile, Jim Wayne's spirits rose as he gazed across the two thousand shaggy backs bearing the JH brand.

Shoving the cows along were the eight young cowboys who had elected to throw in with him on the venture. They were a rollicking, skylarking lot, but every man was a top hand and he felt sure he could count on their loyalty no matter what might happen.

More than half the herd was composed of Lafe Swanson's improved stock, as fine a bunch of cows, Wayne felt sure, as had ever invaded the Trinity River country. The drive

was accomplished smoothly without untoward happenings, and finally the weary
cattle rolled on to the JH range with bel-
lows of relief.

'Darn critters know they're home,' chuckled Ward Handley, who was deftly superin-
tending operations. 'And so are we,' he
added. 'Yep, Jim, we're here to stay. I'm glad
of it, too. Figure it's about time for me to
tie hard and fast. Yep, figure I've got me a
home.'

They found Ellis's three riders all set for a
housewarming.

'Why didn't you stay away?' one lamented.
'We ain't had it so easy in a coon's age.
Nothing to do but eat and sleep and ride
around a bit now and then to say hello to
the critters Higginbottom left when he
pulled out. Incidentally, Jim, they tally quite
a mite more than you figured. With what
you've brought with you, the spread is darn
near stocked as it should be. The calf
round-up next spring will just about do it.

'Yep, things are still jumpy over in town,'
he replied to Wayne's question. 'A lot more
folks have pulled out and more are planning
to go. Stranger dropping in would 'low Fort
Worth is a gone gosling, but Ellis and
Sweatless Sam don't think so. And that
young lawyer, Matt Jarret — he's a hot iron

— he's telling the paper-backs that they're making a big mistake they'll live to regret. I've a notion he's got the right of it. Oh, sure, Sweatless is still doing all right, but most of the other saloons either are boarded up or are showing "For Sale" signs.'

'I think I'll have a talk with Jarret,' Wayne said thoughtfully. A few days later he did so.

'Our pressing problem, Wayne, is the time element,' Jarret explained. 'If the land grant subsidy given by the legislature expires before the road gets here, we're sunk. Something must be done within months. And things are still bad back East — more failures, a tightening of money. The railroad directors appear afraid to move, not knowing if they can corral the needed money to complete the grading of the last twenty-six miles from Eagle Ford here, and being unwilling to gamble on it. That's how the situation stands.'

'Jarret,' Wayne replied, 'we're not licked yet, and as I said once before, we're going to get our railroad if every bank and peanut stand in the entire East fails. That I'll promise you.'

'You restore my confidence,' Jarret said. 'By gosh, we'll do it! Yes, we'll have the laugh on the paper-backs yet. What now?'

'Now I want time to do a little thinking,'

Wayne replied. 'I'm beginning to get a notion that I believe will work. There's no great rush — we have till spring to get going. If the grading from Eagle Ford was completed and the subsidy guaranteed, I think the road officials would hold up their end, don't you?'

'Yes, I do,' said Jarret. 'As I mentioned, the time element is the pressing problem.'

'There'll be all the time we need,' Wayne declared confidently. 'Well, I've got to get back to the spread; I'll see you again before long.'

Wayne twice met Malcolm Otey, the Dallas real estate man, in the course of his visits to town. Otey was cordial, and expressed regret that he had been unable to keep his appointment with Wayne in Dodge City, having been unexpectedly called back to Dallas by urgent business matters. But it seemed to Wayne that his thin smile had a derisive quality as his eyes rested on the boarded-up store fronts and the blank and staring windows.

Not long after his second meeting with Otey, Wayne paid a visit to Matt Jarret. He found the lawyer in a wrathful mood.

'Look at this article in the *Dallas Herald,* written by that blankety-blank Malcolm Otey!' he bawled, shaking the newspaper under Wayne's nose and pointing to the offending article. Wayne accepted the paper and read, among other things:

'Fort Worth is so dead I saw a panther lying asleep and unmolested in the main street.'

'Panther asleep in the main street!' snorted Jarret.

Wayne looked up from the paper and grinned at the wrathful lawyer.

'Matt,' he said, 'the gentleman has unwittingly and unintentionally given us the very ammunition we need.'

'But why did he do it?' asked Jarret. 'He's always seemed friendly towards Fort Worth folks.'

'He has holdings around Dallas, or so I've been given to understand,' Wayne replied. 'And Dallas has always looked on Fort Worth as a potential rival. Otey, not unnaturally, wants all the prosperity of the section centred around Dallas. So he aimed to drive a spike or two in the Fort Worth coffin. I've a notion he'll find he's stirred up a rather lively corpse. Come on; we're going to give this article a mite of circulation. First stop the Western Star. There'll be a good crowd there at this time of evening. I want the folks to give this article the once-over. We'll spread it around.'

They proceeded to do just that, and by so doing they raised a storm. The calumny was greeted with hoots of derision.

'Gents, that blankety-blank has named us,' shouted an old rancher. 'From now on this ain't Fort Worth; this is Panther Town, and panthers have got claws. We'll give those hellions their come-uppance before we're finished with them.'

'But how?' somebody asked.

The rancher jerked his thumb toward Jim Wayne. '*He'll* find a way, you just watch,' he replied. 'I've had my eye on that young feller ever since he showed up in this section. He believes in Fort — I mean Panther Town — and he'll show us how to use our claws. Just you watch!'

CHAPTER TEN

And so the 'Panther City' was born, and Fort Worth got a nickname that would stick. Jeers were hurled at Dallas. To add insult to injury, the fire department bought a panther cub for a mascot and local clubs attached the name 'Panther' to their former titles.

Time passes quickly on the rangeland when one is very busy, and Jim Wayne was actually astonished when he realized that the Texas bluebells and other flowers of spring were flaunting their beauty on the prairie and that the calf roundup was at hand.

Old Ward Handley, already a part owner, rubbed his hands together gleefully after the roundup was over.

'Better'n we expected,' he told Wayne. 'Yep, the tally's way up. We're doing fine, and we'll do a lot better after that dad-gummed railroad gets here and makes shipping easy. Town's sorta lonesome right now, though!'

Fort Worth was indeed beginning to look unpleasantly like a ghost town. The population had shrunk from over five thousand to less than a thousand; but the thousand were stalwart diehards who still had faith in the Panther Town's future. And Jim Wayne knew it was time for the Panthers to sharpen their claws. He rode in for a talk with Matt Jarret, and they discussed the matter pro and con.

'First we'll go see the Governor and try and enlist his support, which we will need,' Wayne said. 'I feel he'll see things our way. I'll meet you here in the morning.'

Early the following day they set out on the two-hundred-mile ride to Austin, the state capital.

In Austin, they had no difficulty obtaining an appointment with the state's chief executive.

The Governor, a genial, alert man with progressive ideas, listened courteously to what they had to say. After Wayne had finished outlining his plan, he sat silent for some moments, drumming on his desk with his fingertips and gazing out the window. Finally he turned to the young rancher with a smile.

'Okay, Mr. Wayne, I'll string along with

you,' he said. 'I think your notion is a good one and well worth putting to the test. You can count on my support; I hope to be able to swing the legislators, or enough of them, into line and prevent an early adjustment. But I warn you there will be opposition that will make your task more difficult. Some of the methods they may employ to delay you will be unorthodox, to put it mildly.'

'I think we will be able to cope with unorthodox methods,' Jim predicted grimly.

Looking at him, the Governor felt that the statement was not born of over-confidence.

'I'll give you a letter to a Texas & Pacific official here in the capital,' he said. 'It may help to smooth the trail for you. Good luck with your project, Mr. Wayne. I heartily approve of it.'

They contacted the official in question. After reading the Governor's letter, he in turn got in touch by wire with his colleagues in the East. The consultation lasted all day. Finally an agreement was reached. Fort Worth would grade the remaining twenty-six miles of unfinished roadbed from Eagle Ford in exchange for a lien on the road.

Wayne and Jarret carried the word to Fort Worth, where it was received with enthusiasm. The Panthers, their claws sharpened to razor edge, got busy to complete the moribund railroad, and the dirt flew. Every available man was pressed into service. Business establishments and spreads operated with skeleton forces and sent the bulk of their help to the railroad right-of-way to wield pick and shovel. The women of the city worked in relays, preparing coffee and food and feeding and watering the mules.

There were blistered hands, sunburn, aching backs and sore feet a-plenty. The toilers cursed the heat, the flies, Malcolm Otey and the day they were born, but stuck stubbornly to the chore. And the raw scar of newly turned earth crept steadily westward across the prairie, with the twin steel ribbons flowing close behind.

Jim Wayne was everywhere, directing, encouraging, doing the work of two men. Recognizing him as the moving spirit of the project, the road builders had dubbed him the Old Man, a term of highest respect, pinned only on a boss who is liked and admired.

'Knows more about it than anybody else,' was the consensus of opinion. 'A nice jigger, but plenty salty if necessary. Understand he could cut five notches on the handles of those big guns he always packs, if he was the sort to cut notches. Handy with his fists, too. A plumb nice jigger, but wouldn't want to get him riled. That big feller Ellis, who's always close to Wayne, is another salty one, but he's a worker, too.'

Wayne wore his guns all the time, for he had not forgotten the Governor's warning. What anybody could do to slow up the work he had not the slightest notion, but he was taking no chances.

He had seen nothing of Malcolm Otey since his return from the capital, and he wondered how the real estate man was taking it. Philosophically, no doubt, hoping that the grading would not be completed in time.

Wayne grimly admitted to himself that Otey had reason to hope and to develop a sanguine feeling. The race was so tight that only a few days' delay would drop the balance against the Panthers. He redoubled his efforts and prayed that the good weather would continue. A spell of hard rain would slow operations badly, and the line between victory and defeat was fast becoming a hairline.

And then he got a disturbing report from Val Rader, in charge of the right-of-way patrol.

'Know that long brush-covered ridge to the south?' he said. 'Well, there's been a couple of hellions holed up in the brush there all day. They were trying to stay out of sight, but I spotted them. They were keeping tabs on the work, all right, no doubt as to that. I've no notion what they might have in mind, but I'm ready to swear it's something. They weren't hanging out there all day just to admire the scenery. Wonder what they *could* have in mind?'

Wayne wondered, too, and racked his brains for a solution. As he concentrated on the problem, his gaze drifted to the hissing locomotive that transported the ties and rails. The T. & P., because of its financial difficulties, was woefully short of rolling stock; and that engine, Wayne knew, was the only one available at the moment. If something should happen to it, they were sunk.

Quickly Wayne arrived at a decision. 'Val,' he said, 'get in touch with your night guards and have them hole up here as soon as it gets dark. I'll be here with them.'

'So will I,' the range boss stated cheerfully. 'Wouldn't want to miss anything.'

'But you've been up since daylight,' Wayne demurred.

'Don't rec'lect you snoozin' under a tree,' Rader replied. 'I'm stayin'.'

'Okay,' Wayne agreed. 'Maybe we can catch a wink or two while the boys keep an eye on things.'

Nightfall found three of the Boxed E rannies and Craig Hoyt on duty; the latter had quit his job with Lafe Swanson to ride for the JH.

'May be nothing to it; maybe I'm just imagining things,' Wayne told them. 'But it does look funny that somebody should be keeping tabs on us all day. So we'll just hope there'll be no trouble and be ready for it if it comes.'

'Hope it does come,' said Val Rader. 'All day I've had an itch to plug somebody. Been a long time since I collected me a scalp. I gotta catch up with Jim; he got two up at Dodge City and I only got one.'

The hands made themselves as comfortable as circumstances and conditions allowed, behind heaps of earth and stacks of cross-ties. Their position was good, in that they could spot anything crossing the open prairie for quite some distance, even in the dim starlight. There were no thickets or other stands of growth within a couple of hundred yards of the right of way.

Wayne told the engine watchman what was suspected. He did not appear particularly perturbed.

'That so?' replied the old man. 'Some scalawags got notions to do things to my baby, eh?' He patted the Russian-iron sheathing of the boiler head. 'They might get a surprise. Okay, Boss-man, I'll stay inside the cab. As you say, I'll be safer there than any place else. I'll hop up there in a minute or two. Got a little chore to do down here first.'

Wayne left him pottering with something around the lower section of the boiler.

Confident that the old fellow would come to no harm, no matter what developed, Wayne returned to his men, who were smoking cigarettes with the glowing tips carefully screened and conversing in low tones.

'If a raid is attempted, I figure it will come from the south. But keep an eye on the north, too, just in case,' he told them. 'I don't think anything will happen before midnight at the earliest, so I'll try and knock off an hour or two of shuteye. Wake me if you hear or see anything.'

Before lying down, he took a last look around. Everything appeared to be under control. The horses had been concealed in a thicket some distance back along the right of way and to the north, where it was highly unlikely that anybody would stumble on to them. Down the track a little way loomed the black bulk of the engine, the steam in its boiler purring softly. Uncle Zeke, the watchman, would be stretched out on the floor of the cab, where he would be in little danger from flying lead should some happen to come his way.

For two hours and more, Wayne slept soundly, awaking much refreshed.

'Nothing so far,' said Rader. 'Say! That engine watchman, Uncle Zeke, is a prime old feller. A little while ago he snuk over here with a pot of hot coffee he'd made on a shovelful of coals in the cab. We saved some for you.'

The night was very still, with only an occasional weird cry of some bird to break the silence. The stars were dimmed somewhat by a film of cloud, but objects were visible for some distance across the prairie.

The great clock in the sky wheeled westward. Wayne was beginning to believe that their fears were groundless when Rader suddenly spoke in a whisper.

'I hear horses coming up from the south,' he breathed. Wayne strained his ears, and a moment later he also heard the faint patter that swiftly grew louder. A few more minutes and the sound abruptly ceased.

'They're behind that stand of brush over there,' murmured Rader, gesturing to the dark mass of a thicket a couple of hundred yards distant. 'Guess they're leaving their cayuses. Look out! Here they come.'

He was right. Nearly a dozen shadowy shapes were stealing across the prairie towards the dark bulk of the locomotive.

'Hold it a minute,' Wayne whispered. 'Let them get a little closer. We'll give them a chance, more'n they'd give us.' Another moment, and his voice rang out:

'Elevate! You're covered!'

CHAPTER ELEVEN

The advancing shapes halted. Wayne saw the gleam of shifted metal and fired at the faint glimmer. One of the shapes pitched forward and lay still. Beside him, Rader's gun boomed. Another of the raiders whirled sideways and went down. The night fairly exploded to a bellow of six-shooters. A third raider fell. The others dived behind the embankment and fired over its lip. The cowboys crouched low, shooting at the flashes.

Back and forth gushed the lances of orange flame. The air quivered to the reports. Geysers of earth spurted up from slugs fired low. Others whined past. But both sides were pretty well under cover. It looked as if the battle would continue all night, for neither side dared leave their shelter.

'Say! I don't like this,' Rader exclaimed. 'Looks like those hellions are sorta fightin' a delaying action. May be some more of them about. If they circle around and get behind us, we'll be caught in a crossfire.' He glanced apprehensively to the north.

Jim Wayne had already thought of that and experienced a cold feeling along his backbone. He opened his lips to speak, when suddenly there was a hissing roar from the direction of the locomotive, followed instantly by yells of pain. Into the open burst the raiders, bawling curses, fleeing madly back the way they came. Rader's gun banged, and one flipped over like a plugged rabbit. Before his companions, astonished by the unexpected happening, could get into action, the darkness had swallowed the band. A moment later the beat of fast hoofs sounded, fading away into the south.

Val Rader gave an exultant howl. 'I got me two, and Jim only got one!' he whooped. 'That makes us even. What in blazes happened? I thought the blasted engine had blown up.'

'I'm getting a notion, but first let's make sure there's no life in those carcasses,' Wayne replied.

They advanced on the bodies cautiously, guns ready for instant action, but there was no need for prudence. All four raiders were satisfactorily dead.

'We'll make a light and examine them later,' Wayne said. 'Right now I want to see Uncle Zeke.'

They found Uncle Zeke leaning against a drive wheel, smoking a corncob pipe. In his hand was a length of hose.

'See that gedunkus down there by the belly of the b'iler?' he replied to the questions volleyed at him. 'That's what we calls a mud valve. Mud in the water settles on to the crown sheet and into the belly of the b'iler. So every now and then we opens that valve and blows out the mud. Plenty of steam and hot water comes out with the mud. A while back I figured a way to fasten this hose to the valve and wash the dust off my baby fast. So tonight I hooked her up. Figured she might come in handy. And when I saw those scalawags were holed up behind the embankment, where you folks couldn't reach 'em with your guns, I gave them a sprinkling with b'ilin' water. Figured that with a hundred and fifty pounds pressure on the gauge I could reach 'em. Guess I did.'

'You sure did!' whooped Val Rader. 'Reckon the blankety-blanks figured they were caught in a rainstorm in hell.'

The cowboys roared with laughter. They clapped Uncle Zeke on the back, and each

111

solemnly shook hands with him.

'Well,' said Wayne, 'it looks like most of the credit for this night's work goes to Uncle Zeke. And, Uncle Zeke,' he added, 'if you ever get tired of railroading, my cook is an old Mexican jigger who can stand some help in the kitchen.'

'Boss man, I'd sure like that,' replied Uncle Zeke. 'I worked on a spread over on the Louisiana side when I was a young feller, and I sorta got a hankering to get back to cow raisin'. I like my baby here, but I miss my horse.'

'Fine!' said Wayne. 'We'll have a talk and work things out tomorrow. Now let's get a fire going and give those bodies a once-over.'

The fire was kindled, the bodies dragged into the circle of light. They were ornery-looking specimens that nobody recognized. Their pockets yielded nothing of significance save a surprisingly large amount of money.

'Betcha they're part of the bunch you tangled with there by the Cimarron, Jim,' said Rader. 'Hired guns, that's what they were. Look at their hands. They haven't done a day's work in a coon's age, but they were loaded. What shall we do with the dinero, Jim?'

'Divide it up among you,' said Wayne. 'You can use it better'n the county treasurer, where it'll go if the sheriff gets his paws on it. Come here, Uncle Zeke, and get your divvy.'

'Yes, hired guns; I know the sort,' repeated Rader, shoving coin and bills into his pocket. 'But who the devil hired 'em?'

'That's what I'd like to know,' Wayne said grimly. 'Well, I'm going to try and get a little more sleep; no sense in riding to town at this time of night. You'd better lie down, too, Val.'

As an afterthought, Wayne ordered a search of the thicket where the raiders had evidently left their horses before advancing on foot, against the chance that the cayuses belonging to the dead men had been left behind. Brands might tell something.

However, no horses were found; they had apparently followed the others.

Great was the excitement of the graders when they arrived to take up the day's work. Wayne was congratulated, and praised for his acumen. They wanted to praise Uncle Zeke, too, but he was asleep and Wayne wouldn't allow him to be awakened.

'You can talk to him this evening,' he told the well-wishers.

The sheriff was notified and took care of

the bodies. 'Oh, sure we'll hold an inquest,' he said. 'No sense in it, but the coroner figures he has to do something to earn his pay.

'You sure saved the bacon, Jim,' he added. 'If they'd grabbed the engine they could have drained the boiler, built up a fire and melted her down. That would have been the finish. They'd never have gotten another one here in time. Going to be close as it is.'

Wayne knew it. It was going to be too close for comfort. Ominous news had come from the capital; the legislature was hurrying towards adjournment, before which date the work had to be completed or all that had been accomplished would go for naught. He sent Matt Jarret, the lawyer, riding at top speed to call on the Governor.

'Maybe the Governor can hold the legislature until the work is completed,' he said to Ran Ellis. 'All we need now is a few more days.'

'We'll do it,' declared Ellis.

'But why didn't you tip me off to what was building up the other night?' he added in injured tones. 'I missed all the fun.'

'I would have if you hadn't had to ride back to your spread in the early afternoon,' Wayne replied. 'I didn't get the notion until Val Rader told me of those hellions keeping tabs on us from the ridge.'

'Val's sorta put out, too, because you wouldn't let him take scalps,' Ellis said.

'I think he was joking,' Wayne smiled.

'I'm not so sure,' Ellis disagreed. 'I got my suspicions of that quarter-Injun. Wouldn't be surprised if he's got a collection of hair tucked away some place.'

With the day of doom fast approaching, the Panthers redoubled their efforts. A night shift, working by lantern and flare light, was added. Hardly anybody got more than four hours' sleep a night, and the dirt really flew.

Matt Jarret got back from the capital with word that the Governor was doing all he could to hold the legislature in session, but advised the graders to stir their stumps. He said that interests were pulling wires and working on individual legislators.

'We'll do it,' Jim Wayne repeated. The sweating toilers roared agreement and scratched gravel.

Now the buildings of Fort Worth were to be seen. With their goal in plain sight, the Panthers did the impossible and speeded up still a little more. Shovels scraped and clattered, and picks chunked into the stubborn earth. Mauls described flaming arcs and thudded solidly on to spike heads. Close on the heels of the pick and shovel men rumbled the cars loaded with cross-ties, rails, bolts and fish plates. The engineer leaned out of his cab and bellowed encouragement.

'Drill, ye terriers, drill!' he shouted.

The exhaust boomed and the side rods clanked; the ponderous drive wheels ground the rails; air hissed through the port as he slammed on the brakes and brought his clanging charges to a halt, seemingly on the very brink of disaster. 'Drill, ye terriers, drill!'

The patrol heightened its vigilance, and the word went out that any stranger approaching the grade would be shot, no questions asked. Nobody approached.

There was golden sunshine and a sky of blue the day the final rail chunked on to the ties. The spike mauls thudded. Ran Ellis waved something in the air.

'We haven't any golden spike like the one they used when the Union Pacific and the Central Pacific met in Utah,' he shouted, 'but here's a nugget I saved as a souvenir. Hammer it in with the last one.'

The last spike was driven, with the soft gold of the nugget clamped around its head, to the accompaniment of thunderous cheers. Legislative adjournment was still a day off.

116

The first train into Fort Worth stopped at what would later be Boaz Street and Lancaster Avenue, its whistle cord tied down and Jim Wayne and the editor of the local paper franctically stuffing fuel into the firebox to keep the steam pressure up and the whistle going.

That night the Panthers celebrated as never before. And they had good reason to celebrate. They had done the impossible. They had their railroad — on time!

CHAPTER TWELVE

Almost overnight, Fort Worth became a wild frontier town.

Solid citizens of Fort Worth, among them Sweatless Sam, sensed the value of capitalizing on the town's strategic location as the market place of the great south-western empire of cattle and cattlemen. They went forward with plans to organize a meat-packing company and build a stockyard. Real estate values rose a little more.

'I've had half a dozen offers for my establishment,' chuckled Sweatless Sam. 'If I wasn't satisfied with a substantial well-paying business that'll keep on going throughout the years, I'd have been tempted to accept one.'

'You're right,' replied Jim Wayne. 'What a lot of folks don't appear able to realize is that this boom won't last for ever. After a while the construction camps will move west and Fort Worth will settle down to a normal prosperity based on a steady growth and development. But while it lasts she'll whoop.'

Fort Worth whooped, all right, wallowing in the glamour, excitement and violence of a typical frontier town. Shootings and cuttings became common occurrences, and there were robberies. Cattlemen began complaining of stock losses. And from the South-west rolled the longhorn tide.

For the time being, Jim Wayne was too busy to give much thought to Forth Worth shenanigans. Buildings had to be tightened up, corrals strengthened, and other repairs made against the coming winter. More waterholes were dug, winter forage cut and stowed. Old Higginbottom had let things get a bit run down during the last years of his tenancy. Wayne was a bit reluctant to spare the time, therefore, when Sweatless Sam sent word he wanted to see him.

'Guess I'd better go, though,' he told Ward Handley. 'That old jigger must have something in mind he considers important.'

'Yep, Sweatless has plenty of wrinkles on his horns,' agreed Handley. 'You'd better go; I'll keep things moving while you're gone.'

Wayne found Sweatless ensconced at his usual position near the far end of the bar and close to the till. He shook hands cordially and led the way to an isolated table in a corner. Without preamble, he launched into his reason for summoning the rancher.

'We aim to have our packing establishment and our cattle yard in operation by this fall,' he said. 'We'll be ready for business, and we figure you should get first whack. So we'd like to buy your entire beef this fall, every head you can dig out. Standard market prices; with no shipping costs to divvy up, your profit will be larger than it would be if you shipped East. What do you say?'

'What could I say but agree?' Wayne gratefully accepted the offer. 'Mighty nice of you, Sam.'

'The boys all figure that if it hadn't been for you, Fort Worth would be a gone gosling by now,' said Sweatless. 'They'd like to do a little something to show their appreciation. Good business, too. The critters you brought up from the Nueces country are just about the best beef in this section. We won't lose by it.'

Wayne was truly grateful for the unexpected windfall.

'We'll be sitting pretty for the winter,' he told Handley. 'Now we won't have to worry about money with which to pay wages and buy stuff we need. Sure was fine of the folks.'

'The right sort of folks appreciate what's done for them and don't forget,' said the wise old rannie. 'They know darn well that if it hadn't been for you, things would be pretty bad hereabouts about now. They're glad of a chance to even up the score a mite.'

'We'll comb out everything we can spare,' Wayne decided. 'Looks like the market will be in good shape this fall and prices high. The panic hit a lot of cowmen hard, and there won't be the normal number of critters coming up the trails this year. I'm sure glad I had faith in the Fort Worth section and took a gamble on it.'

'You took advantage of opportunity, that's all,' declared the range boss. 'Seems to me I rec'lect some up-and-coming feller — I can't remember who — said, "Opportunity? I make opportunity!" Reckon that sorta applied to you.'

Wayne chuckled. Napoleon's famous remark sounded a mite out of place coming from Handley's mouth.

A few days later, Ran Ellis rode up to the JH ranch house. His eyes were snapping and he appeared to be in a thoroughly bad temper.

'What's the matter, Ran?' Wayne asked, after he had told Uncle Zeke, now the cook's assistant, to put on coffee and fix a snack.

'I'm losing cows, that's what's the matter,' Ellis declared wrathfully. 'More than a hundred head night before last.'

Wayne looked serious. 'Where'd they go, have you any notion?' he asked. Ellis shrugged his shoulders.

'First to the Cap Rock hills, then west to New Mexico, I reckon,' he replied.

'A long drive,' Wayne commented meditatively.

'Yes, and a mighty sparsely settled country over there, and rough,' Ellis returned. 'The sort of section where folks don't ask questions. Pass what few towns they might come across in the dark and hole up during the day in thickets and groves. It's been done. Anyhow, they went west after they were wide-looped. We tracked 'em for a while, then lost the trail. Kept on going for about twenty miles but couldn't pick it up again. Grass is heavy and springs up again right after it's been beat down. Not even Rader could find a trace of their passing.'

'We've got to put a stop to it,' Wayne said. 'Yours isn't the first complaint I've heard. No doubt but there's a bunch working the section. Must be a well-organized outfit with plenty of savvy, and with access to the market for slick-iron cows. Well, we'll have all to work together and tangle their twine for them before it gets too serious. Their mode of operating is worse in the long run than the spectacular running off of an occasional herd. No rancher can stand that sort of a steady drain on his resources.'

Uncle Zeke called to them to come and get the snack, and for a while they ate in silence.

'By the way,' Ellis suddenly remarked, 'I saw Malcolm Otey in town. He asked about you. Seemed quite chipper and didn't 'pear to hold a grudge.'

'No reason he should,' Wayne said. 'I gather that he has some good investments around Dallas, and Dallas will do all right.'

'I guess that's so,' agreed Ellis. 'Well, thanks for the snack and the swig; both were fine, Uncle Zeke. I'll have to get back to my spread — work to do. Will keep in touch with you, Jim, and I guess we'd better do a mite of night patrol from now on, don't you think so? Right! I'll be seeing you.'

After Ellis departed, Wayne sat for some time smoking and thinking.

Would it be possible, he wondered, to outsmart the rustlers and lure them into the open? For a long time he turned the matter over in his mind and finally evolved a plan

he believed might work. He called in Handley, Craig Hoyt and one or two others and
broached the notion. A lengthy conference
followed.

'I believe it'll work,' declared Handley.
'That sort usually have a weakness: they
don't give other folks credit for much savvy.
I've a notion the sidewinders are due to get
a mite of a surprise.'

That evening several of the JH hands rode
to town. In the saloons they talked loudly of
the sale their boss was making to the packing company, which was common knowledge.

'We aim to start tomorrow and comb out
everything we can tie on to,' he said. 'We'll
hold 'em in loose herd with salt and a little
scattered grain round the waterholes. That
way we'll get a good spot tally before
roundup time.'

So the JH spread became a hive of industry; the thickets and coulees were carefully
combed and the resulting stock loosely
herded about the waterholes or on the
banks of streams.

An exceptionally large bunch was collected near a waterhole not far from the
western edge of the JH holding and well to
the south.

Each evening as twilight began to fall, the

JH hands rode in to the ranch house, leaving the cows to graze. And each night after full dark, furtive riders might have been seen slipping like shadows into the grove near the waterhole.

One of the hands who rode home each evening was keen-eyed Val Rader who, while apparently occupied with routine chores, in reality kept a constant watch on the brush-covered ridges and hillocks to the west.

It was on the third evening, after the herd had gained sizeable proportions, that Rader made his report.

'An hombre's been on that rise to the south-west today, keeping tabs on us,' he told Jim Wayne. 'Did a good chore of keeping under cover, but he forgot bridle irons flash in sunlight. I spotted the flashes. Yep, he was there, all right.'

'Didn't I tell you they'd fall for it?' chortled Ran Ellis. 'I knew darn well they would. Remember me saying, Jim, that not giving the other feller credit for any savvy is an owlhoot weakness. They figure those beefs are duck soup for them. Their mouths must be watering over that herd. Betcha they'll make their try tonight.'

'And tonight I'm going along with you gents,' declared Rader. 'I don't need any sleep! Think I wanta miss out on the fun?'

'By the way, it looks like you're getting neighbours over to the west,' Ellis remarked as they made ready to ride. 'The old Davis place, the Tumbling D. I heard a few months back, when things were on the downgrade, that it had been sold. Bought by some smart jigger who figured conditions would change, I reckon. Just the other day one of the boys riding over that way saw wagons loaded with household truck pulling up to the *casa*.'

'That so?' Wayne asked. 'Reckon I'll have to ride over and pay them a housewarming visit.'

A few minutes later the posse, ten strong, rode south by west across the range.

'In a way, we're taking the law in our own hands, which honest citizens should refrain from doing if possible,' Wayne observed. 'However, in this particular instance, I think we're justified in so doing.'

'You're darned right we are,' growled Ellis. 'We're out to mow down a gang of snake-blooded murderers. I'm willing to bet the last peso I have that it's the same bunch that killed Bob Randolph up by the Red River. And,' he added grimly, 'I'm of a notion that after tonight Bob is going to sleep better.'

There was agreement, and Wayne said nothing more. Flame, his big sorrel, being laid up for a few days with a sore hock, he forked a rangy bay that had speed and endurance.

At the grove, they got the horses tethered and a satisfactory position located at the south edge. The cloud rack had drifted away; the sky was washed clean, the stars brilliant. By their light they could clearly discern the dark blobs that were the leisurely moving cattle.

'A wide-looper's dream,' Ran Ellis chuckled softly. 'Look how they're bunched, with their bellies full. A couple of school kids could move 'em off, easy. Well, guess it'll be a couple of hours before they show, if they are figuring to tie on to 'em tonight. Reckon we can risk a smoke?'

'Okay, but cup your hands over the matches,' Wayne warned.

Cigarettes going, the punchers settled down comfortably to wait. It was a relief when, nearly two hours later, Val Rader suddenly whispered:

'I hear horses!'

CHAPTER THIRTEEN

Louder and louder came the patter of hoofs on the grass. Another moment and vague shapes loomed in the starlight, horsemen converging on the herd. Wayne counted eight altogether.

Closer and closer. Now they were less than a score of yards distant, slowing their pace, beginning to circle the herd.

'Let 'em have it!' roared Ellis, and shot with both hands. The others joined in. The orange flashes lighted the prairie, the trees of the grove, the bawling cattle.

Three saddles were emptied by that first thundering volley, but the outlaws, taken by surprise, nevertheless fought back. Craig Hoyt swore viciously as a bullet sliced his arm. Another tore through the crown of Wayne's hat. Still another burned a red streak across his cheek and nearly knocked him off his feet.

That was too much. He began firing, too.

And even as he pulled the trigger, he saw the man at whom he had aimed whirl sideways from his hull.

Another blast of lead from the grove, and two more wide-loopers fell. Seven riderless horses galloped wildly across the prairie.

But one rider, a tall man forking a black, stayed in the saddle. He whirled his mount and streaked away southward, bending low over the animal's neck. Bullets whipped around him but he was untouched.

'I'll get him! Look after the others!' Wayne shouted. He raced to where his horse was tethered, whipped into the saddle and sent the bay charging in pursuit. The fugitive had a good lead, but was still clearly visible.

Very quickly, however, Wayne realized that the chance of overtaking him was not very good. The bay, while an excellent horse, was not Flame, and the wide-looper was superbly mounted.

Mile after mile flowed back under the flying hoofs, with the black widening the distance little by little. And then Wayne saw, ahead, what appeared to be a vast, nebulous shadow, low down but higher than the prairie floor. For a moment he was at a loss to account for the unexpected manifestation.

Then abruptly he understood. That

shadow was the rank growth which covered the sinister expanse of swampland known as the Big Bottoms. The fugitive was heading straight for the Big Bottoms. Another three minutes and the lurking shadow would swallow horse and rider.

With a disgusted oath, Wayne pulled the bay to a halt and turned around.

He had covered but a few miles of the return trip when he saw three horsemen riding swiftly from the north. He loosened the reloaded Winchester in its sheath and closely watched their approach. Another moment and he recognized Ellis, Rader and Ward Handley.

'Did you get him?' the Boxed E owner called as they drew near. Wayne shook his head.

'Kept in front and went into the Bottoms,' he replied. 'I figured it best not to follow him.'

'You figured right,' said Ellis. 'Nobody unfamiliar with the Bottoms has any business venturing in there, especially at night. If he knows the Bottoms, and it looks like he does, he'd have had you right where he wanted you. Yep, you did right not to follow him. I wouldn't have, and I know the Bottoms better than most. Well, we did a pretty good night's work, anyhow. Seven of the hellions. We didn't wait to take a look at them; figured we'd better hightail after you, just in case. We'll look 'em over when we get back to the grove. The boys began getting the cows quieted down. The ruckus scared the stuffing outa them, but they didn't run; too fat and full, I reckon.'

When they reached the grove, they found the cowboys had kindled a fire and laid out the bodies for inspection.

'Just like the others you and Val downed, they had quite a passel of dinero on them,' Craig Hoyt observed to Wayne. 'There it is by the fire.'

'You take it, Ran,' Wayne said. 'It will partly make up for the cows you lost.' The others added their voices in agreement.

Meanwhile, the sharp-eyed Rader was giving the bodies a careful once-over. He uttered an exclamation of satisfaction.

'I've seen two of 'em in Fort Worth,' he announced. 'This lanky one with the scar over his eye, and the red-headed one. I'll swear to it. Yep, it's the same bunch, sure as shootin'.'

'Tomorrow we'll try and round up the horses,' Wayne said. 'The brands may tell us something, though I doubt it. Anyhow, the rigs must be removed so they won't suffer.'

'What shall we do with the carcasses?' Ellis asked.

'Leave them here and notify the sheriff,' Wayne decided. 'Well, I guess we've done all we can, so let's head for home. Be daylight by the time we get there. My cayuse 'pears to have gotten his wind back and is fit to travel.'

The rose and gold of the dawn was flaming the eastern sky by the time they reached the ranch house and had the horses cared for. Then, thoroughly tired out, everybody went to sleep, Wayne having first instructed one of the hands to ride to town and notify the sheriff.

That worthy arrived at the JH ranch house, along with a deputy and a light wagon, shortly after noon.

'I don't know what I'm getting paid for,' he complained to Jim Wayne. 'You 'pear to be the bully boy with a glass eye as far as law and order hereabouts are concerned. Don't happen to be a Texas Ranger in disguise, do you?'

'I'm afraid I'm not good enough to be a Ranger,' Wayne said in reply.

'I ain't so sure,' differed the sheriff. 'You've sure raised the roof and shoved a chunk under a corner since you coiled your twine here. Well, if somebody will ride along with me to show the way, I'll haul those carcasses to town and lay 'em out for folks to inspect. Yep, we'll have coffee and a snack before we start. How's Uncle Zeke?'

Late that evening, Jim Wayne was told something that caused his brows to draw together in thought.

'We couldn't find hide or hair of 'em,' said one of the hands who had been assigned the chore of rounding up the outlaws' horses. 'Either somebody came and picked 'em up before we got there, or their home pasture ain't overly far off and they headed for it.'

'Sure they weren't holed up in some grove or thicket?'

'We combed 'em all,' the cowboy insisted. 'Nope, they just ain't there.'

Wayne pondered the information and then spoke to Ward Handley.

'It would seem fairly definite that the hangout isn't in the Cap Rock, as we figured it would be,' he told the range boss. 'The horses would never have sought to return that distance.'

'Mighty unlikely they would,' Handley agreed. 'But if it ain't in the Cap Rock, where is it?' Wayne didn't have the answer.

An inquest was held the following day. The coroner's jury justified the killings of the seven wide-loopers and commended Wayne and the others for ridding the community of the pests. Regret was expressed that one had gotten away, and the sheriff was advised to drop a loop on the horned toad as quickly as possible.

Wayne met Malcolm Otey in the Western Star. The real estate man greeted him cordially.

'Still sorry I was unable to keep our appointment that day in Dodge City,' he said. 'I received word of something that required my immediate attention. Doesn't matter; you are fully occupied as it is. I didn't know at the time, of course, that you planned to purchase property here; I had a proposition that I felt might interest you. That's by the board now, of course. You're getting yourself quite a reputation hereabouts, Mr. Wayne,' he added.

'I didn't ask for it,' Wayne replied. Otey smiled, his thin smile that never seemed to reach his eyes.

'Things have a habit of coming to us unrequested,' he said. 'Well, I must go; be seeing you, Mr. Wayne. You were wise to settle in the section.'

He smiled and nodded and departed, and once again Jim Wayne sensed a derisive gleam in the glittering black eyes.

A few days later, since preparations for the coming beef round-up were going smoothly, Wayne decided that a relaxing ride by himself wouldn't be a bad idea.

'I think maybe I'll drop in on our new neighbours over to the west,' he told Ward Handley. 'You know anything about them?'

'Only what I heard in town,' Handley replied. 'Heard an old jigger by the name of Ray from the upper Panhandle bought the spread a while back. Gather he was fed up with Panhandle blizzards and figured down here was a better climate.'

'It is, as I told you once before,' said Wayne. 'They get some lulus in the Panhandle. Okay, I'll be seeing you. Ellis said their *casa* is only a few miles to the west of our holding, and a little to the north, so I may make it over there.'

It was a beautiful day, and Wayne enjoyed his ride across the sun-drenched rangeland.

He veered due north to skirt the end of a wide, deep dry wash that scored the prairie, east and west, for nearly a mile and which he knew was near the western edge of his holdings. Its sides were very steep, grown with thorny mesquite and studded with boulders and loose shale. Its lips were fringed with brush, so that an unwary rider could be almost on top of it before he knew it.

The prairie had been lonely and deserted during the course of his ride, save for clumps of grazing cattle bearing his brand. He was some hundred yards beyond the wash, or arroyo, down which a considerable stream flowed in rainy weather, when from behind a thicket a quarter of a mile or so to the north-west burst a rider mounted on a big raw-boned roan, coming towards him at a prodigious pace.

'That jigger sure has places to go,' he remarked to Flame. Instinctively he loosened the Winchester in its sheath.

'Wonder if somebody's chasing him?' he added. 'Don't see anybody.'

He watched the approaching rider curiously. Abruptly he saw the reason for his breakneck speed. The broken end of a rein jerked and swung from the bit ring, and at each bound of the horse it lashed the frantic animal across the face. The horse, mad with pain and terror, was running away.

The rider, slight of build, was leaning forward, gripping the bit iron, trying vainly to pull the cayuse's head around and bring it to a halt.

'A mite short of muscle,' Wayne commented. 'But that's a powerful critter he's forking.'

Abruptly he let out an alarmed yelp. 'For the love of Pete! It's a girl!'

CHAPTER FOURTEEN

For an instant Jim Wayne stared. Then he realized it was not a sight he could afford to dwell on. The racing horse was headed straight for the brush-grown lip of the dry wash.

'If he goes over that he'll bust his neck and hers, too!' he muttered. His voice rose in a shout.

'Trail, Flame! Trail!'

The great sorrel shot forward, blowing and snorting, his irons drumming the ground. Wayne steered him to cut across the trail of the other horse; but the distance between them was considerable and he was forced to veer Flame more and more towards the devilish wash.

'We'll never do it,' he muttered. 'They'll hit the gully before we reach them.'

'Tumble off!' he shouted to the rider. 'Leave him! Leave him!'

But the girl either could not hear him

above the thunder of the roan's hoofs or didn't understand. She continued to tug at the bit iron, trying to bring the horse's head around.

Wayne set his teeth and urged his mount on with voice and hand. They were almost together now, but the yawning chasm was nearer.

Another urging yell from Wayne. A frantic burst of speed from Flame. He and the roan hit the brush fringing the wash shoulder to shoulder. Wayne threw out a long arm and swept the girl from the saddle just as the roan crashed through the straggle of growth and with a scream went end over end down the side of the draw.

But Flame couldn't stop, either. He went through the brush like a greased pig through a cactus patch. Wayne jammed the girl's face against his breast to protect her from the raking, tearing thorns.

'Take it!' he roared to Flame.

With a squeal and a snort, the sorrel cleared the lip. He landed on bunched feet amid the boulders and shale of the sag, kept his balance by a miracle of agility and went plunging through the flowering weeds and the clawing mesquite. Wayne gripped the girl with one arm and managed to keep Flame's head up with the other.

139

Down they went at a dead run, followed by an avalanche of dust, shale and uprooted boulders. Flame soared over bushes, skittered across sliding shale, cleared juts of rock like an antelope. He reached the bottom of the gulch in a boiling dust cloud and scudded a hundred feet across the dry creek bed before Wayne could bring him to a halt, snorting, blowing, eyes rolling indignantly.

'Blazes, that was close!' his rider panted. 'We were in the air more than on the ground. Horse, you're a wonder!'

Abruptly he realized he had a badly frightened girl in his arms, and that she had not come unscathed from the wild ride down the slope through the thorns and branches. Her shirt was ripped to tatters, and there were long rents in her Levi's. He had shielded her face, and it was untouched, but the rest of her hadn't been so lucky. There were streaks of blood on her white shoulders; others that showed through her torn overalls. Her slender body quivered like an aspen leaf in a gale.

'Take it easy,' he soothed. 'Everything's under control. You're okay now.'

She calmed quickly and looked up into his face with dark blue, astonishingly big eyes. Colour began coming back to her lips and her tanned cheeks. Wayne saw that her hair was short, curly and brown with a glint of red. She was small, and was more than passably pretty. He smiled down at her, his even teeth flashing startlingly white in his bronzed face.

'Quite a ride we had,' he remarked cheerfully. 'But we came out of it top side up, which is more than can be said for your poor cayuse. He's lying over there with a broken neck.'

'And that's where I would be if it weren't for you,' the girl replied, her voice low and soft. 'You were wonderful!'

Wayne grinned. 'Thank my horse,' he said. 'All I did was hang on. Feel better now?'

'Yes, I'm all right now, but heavens, what an experience! Makes one feel as if one would never dare ride again.'

'You'll get over it,' he told her. 'Now I'll put you down for a minute, if you don't mind. I want to make sure my horse didn't suffer any bad cuts.'

He slipped from the saddle and set her on her feet. She glanced down at her clothes and her face flamed scarlet.

'Good heavens!' she gasped. 'I'm a sight!'

'Do those scratches on your shoulders hurt?' Wayne asked.

'They do burn a little,' she admitted.

'Then we'd better take care of them,' he

said. 'Mesquite thorns are poison for some folks, and you might be one of them. I have something in my saddle pouch that should help. Just a minute.'

He gave Flame a quick once-over and decided he had suffered no injuries worth considering. Then from the pouch he took a jar of antiseptic salve which, along with a roll of bandage, he always carried. With it he smeared the red scratches, giving a similar treatment to those showing through the rents in her overalls.

'You mustn't mind,' he said. 'I'm acting as a doctor, you know.'

'I don't mind. It helps a lot, and I thank you,' she said. 'Now give me that jar and I'll look after your poor face. It's raw and bleeding. Does it hurt much?'

'Really, I hadn't noticed; I'm used to scratches,' he disparaged his injuries.

Nevertheless, she insisted on applying the salve, and he found her hands wonderfully deft and gentle.

'Now we're both doctored,' she said, and transferred her attention to her shirt and overalls. 'You don't happen to have a few pins on you? I'm not fit to be seen in daylight.' Wayne shook his head.

'But perhaps some mesquite thorns would serve as a passable substitute. I'll break off a few, if you insist.'

'I do insist,' she replied firmly. 'I'm a disgrace. When my grandfather sees me he'll very likely spank me and put me to bed without any supper.'

'Your grandfather?' Wayne repeated questioningly.

'Yes, Watson Ray. He owns the Tumbling D Ranch to the west of here. We moved down from the Panhandle recently. I'm his granddaughter Gypsy.'

'Gypsy Ray,' he repeated. 'A very pretty name.' He supplied his own.

'And don't worry about your grandfather's reactions,' he consoled her. 'He's evidently an old-timer and will understand.'

Wayne departed, and returned a few minutes later with a handful of the slenderest thorns he could find, which he passed to her. Gypsy busied herself with them and did a fairly creditable job.

When the last thorn was in place Wayne suggested, 'Well, I guess we'd better be heading for your *casa*. I think we can get out of this gully over to the west. A notion the sides aren't so steep there. You can send somebody for your rig. Nothing to do for the horse.'

'The poor thing,' she sighed, and abruptly her big eyes were a trifle misty. Wayne hastened to change the subject.

'Mind if I hold you in front of me?' he asked. 'Flame will pack double better that way.'

'Like you held me coming through the bushes?' She smiled. 'I'm sure I'll be comfortable that way, and I'll feel safer after the scare I got. You don't mind?'

For an answer he mounted, reached down and swung her up in front of him.

It took considerable time to find a spot where they could negotiate the slope. After that an hour elapsed before they sighted a small white ranch house set in a grove of cottonwoods. Seated on the veranda was a big, grizzled old man who brought the legs of his chair to the floor with a thump, his eyes widening.

'Gypsy!' he called apprehensively. 'What's the matter? Are you hurt?'

'I'm fine, Grandpa,' she reassured him as she slipped to the ground and ran lithely to the steps. Seeing she was all right, his face cleared of concern. He stared in astonishment at the condition of her clothes, and his faded blue eyes twinkled.

'Well! well!' he rumbled. 'Looks like you put up a good fight, honey, but reckon you lost in the end. Who is this masterful gent?'

'He's Mr. Jim Wayne, and if it wasn't for

him, I'd be dead,' she answered.

'Dead!' Ray repeated, his face mirroring concern again. 'What do you mean?'

The story of the incident came out with a rush, and it lost nothing in the telling. When Gypsy paused, breathless, old Watson strode down the steps to Wayne, who had dismounted, and held out a gnarled hand.

'Guess all I can say, son, is that I'm mighty, mighty heavy in your debt,' he said, his voice shaking a little. 'She's the only close kin I got in the world, and I think a lot of her.

'Come in, come in,' he added, after they had shaken hands. He let out a whoop, and a wrangler came running to take charge of Flame. They entered the living-room of the ranch house together.

CHAPTER FIFTEEN

'Heard your name mentioned in town,' Ray observed as they sat down. Gypsy had gone upstairs to change. ' 'Pears you're largely responsible for Fort Worth being a going concern again, judging from what folks says.'

'I'm your neighbour to the east, the JH,' Wayne deftly changed the subject. 'Understand you came down from the Panhandle country, sir.'

'That's right,' replied Ray. 'Got fed up with the weather there and scouted around down here when things were sorta mixed up and land values dropping. Found I could buy this holding cheap and tied on to it. Just got my affairs all straightened out and moved in a couple of weeks back.'

'You evidently also had faith in the Fort Worth country,' Wayne observed. Ray nodded.

'Figured it would just be a matter of time,'

he replied. 'Could hardly be otherwise, the section being naturally what it is. I'm getting along in years and don't hanker any more to get rich quick, like younger fellers do. Things hereabouts didn't look so good, though, till you took a hand. Understand you gave a bunch of cow thieves their comeuppance the other night; a good chore. Been having much trouble of that sort?'

'Not overly much,' Wayne answered. 'There have been some losses, but so far not too serious.'

'Give the buckaroos another dose like they got the other night and they'll fight shy of this section,' Ray predicted.

'I hope so,' Wayne said. 'You making out all right, getting settled and so on?'

'Yep, doing okay,' Ray replied. 'I'm pretty well satisfied with my holding. Got a rather nice head of stock, and half a dozen good hands riding for me. Sorta getting on in years, like myself, but they know their business. Got a good cook, too, as I've a notion you'll agree after you sample what he dishes up. Pretty near time to eat.'

At that moment Gypsy reappeared, tripping gracefully down the stairs. She wore something cool and fluffy that enhanced her charm.

She blushed prettily under the admiration

of his regard and lowered her long black lashes that reminded him of the shadow of black lace under candlelight.

A little later the Tumbling D riders trooped in for supper. None was young, but they were alert and efficient-looking. They shook hands warmly, and when Gypsy recounted her experience and the part Wayne had played, they were loud in their acclaim.

'We've watched her grow up from a tad,' Purdy, the range boss, told Wayne as he walked out back with them to wash up before eating. 'And the Old Man sure dotes on her. It hit him mighty hard when his only son died, around ten years back, when Gypsy was only about nine — her mother died when she was born — and I reckon he sorta clung to her and they helped each other forget their loss. He'll never forget what you did today, and if you ever need a helping hand or somebody to back you up in something, no matter what, he'll be right there with bells on. And that goes for the rest of us, too.'

'Thank you,' Wayne said simply. 'It was really a pleasure to have the opportunity to do it.'

The range boss cast him a sideways glance and chuckled.

'Yep, your face looks like you must have had a real nice time,' he said. 'And I figure it's up to us fellers to buy you a new shirt; that one is a mite airy.'

Wayne laughed.

Having washed up as well as conditions permitted, he repaired to the dining-room with Purdy and enjoyed a really excellent supper. He was ready to agree with Ray that the Tumbling D cook knew his business.

Afterwards they sat in the living-room and talked, Wayne familiarizing his host with conditions in the section. Finally old Watson stood up, yawned, stretched, and said:

'You young folks can sit up all night and jabber if you've a mind to, but I'm going to bed. You won't spend the night, Jim?'

'I told my range boss that I didn't expect to be out late, and if I don't show up tonight he'll worry,' Wayne replied. 'But I'll be seeing you soon.'

'Do that,' said Ray, and lumbered up the stairs.

When Wayne reached the JH *casa* he found Handley waiting up for him.

'Was beginning to get a mite bothered,' said the range boss. 'Was afraid you might have run into something. Say! you did run into something. Look at your face! What happened?'

'I ran into a gal,' Wayne replied.

Handley surveyed him searchingly. 'Hmmm!' he said. 'She sure did a good chore on you. Some claws she's got! But what female hasn't?' added the confirmed bachelor of fifty and better. 'What the devil did happen, Jim?'

Wayne told him. Handley shook his grey head and clucked.

'Mighty lucky for the poor kid you happened along when you did,' he said. 'I had much the same thing happen to me once, only I didn't have to try and jump a dry wash. Funny, ain't it, how a horse, usually sensible enough, will panic over a little thing like that? Let a loose strap smack him across the eyes a couple of times and he's liable to go plumb loco. And a horse scared and running away holds its head straight to the front. Pulling it around by the bit iron, which of course will cause it to break its stride and stop, is a chore for a strong man.'

Wayne nodded sober agreement. 'Yes, it was lucky the way things worked out,' he admitted. 'She could hardly have escaped serious injury if she'd gone into the wash when the horse fell.'

'What do you think of our new neighbour?' Handley asked.

'He's okay,' Wayne replied. 'A fine old jigger. I like him. Will have to drop in on him again soon.'

The wise old range boss smiled under his moustache, but did not comment.

Wayne stood up, flexing his long arms. 'I'm going to bed,' he announced. 'I'm beginning to feel as if I'd been drug through a cactus patch and hung on a barbed wire fence to dry.'

'And sleep late,' Handley advised. 'Everything is under control, and we're getting all set for the roundup. No need for you to be up early.'

'Okay, I'll do that,' Wayne replied. 'Good night, Ward.'

More tired than he thought, he did sleep late, and if he dreamed of wide blue eyes and dark brown hair with glints of red, he didn't tell anybody about it when he awoke, close to noon.

He enjoyed a leisurely breakfast, chatted with Uncle Zeke and the cook for a while, then smoked in the living-room, pondering recent events.

Abruptly he reached a decision. Getting the rig on Flame, he rode south by slightly west. After a while he passed the waterhole where the ruckus with the wide-loopers had occurred. Drawing rein, he sat gazing into the south-west. Then he rode on south, but veering to the east, following as nearly as he could the route taken by the fleeing outlaw the night of the waterhole fight.

Mile after mile he rode at a steady pace, until upon the southern horizon loomed that dark, mysterious shadow which was the swamplands of the Big Bottoms.

Still he did not pause, although he was already beyond the point where he had given up the chase of the owlhoot, but continued until he was within a few hundred yards of the first straggle of rank growth that was the outpost of the Big Bottoms. There he drew rein for a moment, studying the terrain.

Where he sat his horse, the grass was heavy and tall, but near where the swamp growth began, it was sparse and the ground appeared to be soft.

Closer investigation showed it was soft, with only scattered tufts of grass. The belt appeared to extend indefinitely.

'Up on the grassland passing cows would leave no mark, but down here, if they crossed this way, there should be an occasional hoof-print,' he remarked to Flame. 'Horse, I'm playing a hunch, and I got a notion it's a straight one.'

He started moving again, riding parallel

to the growth, carefully studying the soil over which he passed. He was headed almost due east and knew he had passed beyond the east limits of his own holding and was on state land south of the Boxed E range. Ellis's ranch house was miles to the north.

He had covered a couple of miles and a part of a third when he found what he sought. Scoring the soft ground were the prints of cattle, a number of them; of horses, too. His pulses quickened.

'Horse, I was right,' he said. 'Ellis's wide-looped cows never went west to the Cap Rock. They laid a false trail, then doubled back and entered the Bottoms. Why? Perhaps to lie low until the pursuit was abandoned, then go west again. But I don't think so. Back somewhere in the Bottoms, perhaps, is a hidden hole-up where they could be held until it was advisable to run them east to the much nearer Louisiana line. I've a strong notion that's the answer. Well, we'll try and find out. Should be easy enough to track in there.'

It wasn't. He had penetrated the swamp only a few hundred yards when he found the ground covered by a film of water. Glassy, opaque, it stretched in every direction as far as the eye could reach. It was not deep, only a few inches, but deep enough to hide all traces of passage on the part of cows or horses. And here the growth was sparse, consisting mostly of fairly tall trees, so that there were no snapped twigs or branches to guide the rider.

'But it's got to end somewhere, so we'll keep going,' he told Flame, who snorted disgustedly and sloshed on through the muck.

They had achieved perhaps a quarter of a mile of dreary progress when, without warning, Flame's forelegs plunged downward, to the fetlock, to the knee, almost to his barrel. He screamed with fright and struggled madly to get back on solid ground. Wayne unforked and added his strength to the horse's frantic efforts.

They made it, but not easily, for the mud clung to Flame's forelegs like the tentacles of an octopus. With all four feet on comparatively solid ground again, he stood shivering and snorting and rolling apprehensive eyes.

That was enough for Wayne. Without ado he mounted and rode back the way he had come. Nor did he pause until he was well out on the grassland. The infernal quagmire was a death trap to anyone unfamiliar with its vagaries.

'But just the same I'm willing to bet it's

possible to run a herd in there,' he told the still nervous horse.

After giving the animal time to catch its breath and recover from its fright, he rode up a slope to the crest of a nearby ridge. Hooking one long leg comfortably over the saddle horn, he rolled a cigarette and gazed across the vast morass, which now appeared even more ominous in the light of the setting sun.

Wayne experienced a compelling urge to ride back into the dark fastnesses of the watery wasteland, to defy its threat and batter down its opposition.

'Okay, but not tonight,' he said aloud, and resolutely faced to the north.

CHAPTER SIXTEEN

It was late when he reached the ranch house, and it took quite a bit of work with currycomb and brush to rid Flame of the swampland mud. The chore completed and all the sorrel's wants provided for, he entered the *casa* by the back, where a light burned, and found Uncle Zeke dozing in a corner of the kitchen.

'Stayed up to keep your supper warm for you,' the coloured man explained.

'Thank you, Uncle Zeke, I appreciate it,' Wayne replied. 'I am as hungry as a prairie wolf in a blizzard.'

'Soon take care of that,' Uncle Zeke said cheerfully. 'Chicken and dumplin's in the pot, and cawn pone in the oven. Comin' right up! Comin' right up!'

'Now sit down and have coffee with me while I eat,' Wayne invited, when the viands were on the table.

'Reckon that's why everybody likes you so

much, Mistuh Jim,' Uncle Zeke said as he poured a cup. ' 'Cause you're always nice to everybody.'

'I'm afraid that's putting it a mite strong, but I try to do the best I can.' Wayne smiled.

'Which is all anybody can do,' said Uncle Zeke, stirring his coffee and adding more sugar.

After a while Wayne pushed back his empty plate, rolled a cigarette and glanced at his table companion.

'Uncle Zeke,' he asked, 'do you know anything about the Big Bottoms?'

'Guess I know about as much as most,' replied the coloured man. 'I was brought up alongside the Bottoms and snuk around in them a lot. Why you ask, Mistuh Jim?'

'Because,' Wayne said slowly, 'I'd like to go in there, if I could find somebody who'd show me how to do it without getting drowned in mud.'

Uncle Zeke rolled his eyes. 'You ain't scared of the haunts and the cunjer folks?'

'I don't think I am,' Wayne replied.

'Nope, guess you're not,' said Uncle Zeke. 'You know why? 'Cause your heart is clean. Man with a clean heart don't need to be afraid of haunts or swamp devils or Old Scratch himself. They know they can't do nothing to a man with a clean heart and don't even try.'

'Thank you, Uncle Zeke,' Wayne said.

'But that don't mean you ain't s'posed to be scared of the Bottoms,' Uncle Zeke added. 'If you don't know 'em and go fooling around 'em, they'll git you.'

'So I learned this afternoon,' Wayne replied dryly.

'You mean to tell me you went in there?' Uncle Zeke asked incredulously.

'I tried to,' Wayne admitted. 'But all of a sudden my horse sank in a mudhole almost up to his withers. I thought for a minute we were both goners.'

Uncle Zeke clucked in his throat and wagged his head. 'You're mighty lucky to get out alive,' he said. 'How come you did a fool thing like that?'

'I was following, or trying to follow, a herd of cows and some horses that did go in there,' Wayne answered. Uncle Zeke nodded.

'Yep, cows and horses could go in, if the folks riding the horses knew what they were about,' he said. 'You got to know where to keep close to the trees, and where to stay away. You got to know what's good ground and what ain't. When there's water on the ground, you got to know what how it looks means. Where there's bad mud under the

158

water, it's black as I am, but where there's good solid clay underneath, it's sorta greyish. There's just some of the things you got to know if you want to go into the Bottoms and come out alive.'

'Sounds like considerable of a chore,' Wayne remarked.

'Oh, it ain't so bad if you've got the know-how,' Uncle Zeke said. 'You really want to go in there, Mistuh Jim?'

'I'd sure like to,' Wayne admitted.

'Well, the haunts and swamp devils didn't get me before, and I reckon they won't now,' replied Uncle Zeke. 'I'll go in there with you, Mistuh Jim; we'll make out.'

'That would be mighty fine of you,' Wayne said gratefully. 'But first I've got to tell you, we might run into something a lot worse than haunts or swamp devils. I've a notion the bunch that tried to wide-loop our cows the other night have a hangout there.'

Uncle Zeke shrugged. 'Done traded lead with cow thieves. Never got hit.'

Wayne chuckled. 'Uncle Zeke,' he said suddenly, 'did you ever hear of Cullen Barnet?'

'Yep, I done heard tell of him,' Uncle Zeke replied. 'Folks say he holed up in the Bottoms, but that was after my time there.'

'There are folks who say he's returned to

the Bottoms, after being away a few years; that he wasn't killed there, as some believe.'

'Wouldn't be surprised,' said Uncle Zeke. ' 'Pears he was a mighty bad man, ornery, plumb hard to kill. And they say he knowed the Bottoms as nobody else ever knowed 'em. Reckon he'd feel safe there. Yep, could be ol' Cullen's come back. But he's just another man with the forked end down and a hat on top. I don't pay Cullen Barnet no mind.'

'I'm beginning to believe you don't pay anybody much mind,' Wayne chuckled.

Uncle Zeke smiled. 'Mistuh Jim, when the Good Lawd gets ready for me, He'll send for me, and not before, so I ain't worryin'.'

And that, Wayne thought, was as fine an expression of faith as he had ever heard.

Two days later, Wayne and Uncle Zeke rode south by slightly east. They started early in the morning and rode slowly, pausing to inspect various preparations for the roundup, conversing with the riders scattered over the range.

'We want to make it look like we're not headed for any place in particular, just on a tour of inspection,' Wayne explained to his companion. 'It's just possible that somebody may be keeping tabs on us — and if we're spotted entering the Bottoms we might find ourselves wearing a tail, with unpleasant consequences.'

'That's right,' agreed Uncle Zeke. 'I got a notion that we're up against some mighty smart scalawags. Yep, we gotta keep our eyes skun.'

So the afternoon was well along when they finally turned east on the state land south of the JH. Wayne constantly scanned their surroundings, but the rangeland stretched lonely and deserted, with no indication of spying eyes following their progress.

'I think we're in the clear,' he said. 'Just a couple more miles, now, to where I found the hoof-marks leading into the swamp.'

A little later he announced, 'Here it is, where they turned into the Bottoms.' He drew rein and for some minutes studied the terrain for as far as the eye could reach. Reassured that it was utterly devoid of human life, he headed Flame for the straggle of lush growth, Uncle Zeke riding beside him. A few more minutes and they were in the gloom of the morass.

Now Uncle Zeke took the lead, pacing his horse slowly, studying the film of water through which they sloshed.

'Must be getting close to where I went into the mudhole,' Wayne observed. Uncle

Zeke nodded and slowed his mount's gait still more. Abruptly he pulled to a halt.

'Uh-huh, here's where you went in,' he said. 'And you were mighty, mighty lucky, to get out. See how black the water over there is; blacker than we've been going through.'

Peering close, Wayne could see that the colour of the water ahead was slightly different and had an oily look.

'If your horse had gotten all four feet in it he never would have gotten out,' added Uncle Zeke. 'And you'd have gone down trying to help him. Mud under that water is just like quicksand. You had a mighty close call, Mistuh Jim. That's devil water over there. Makes me sometimes half think it's alive.'

Wayne got something of the same feeling as he gazed at the turgid, opaque expanse that stretched motionless in the gloom of the trees. It did look almost alive and seemed to leer at him with a derisive gleam, a derisive gleam that somehow was vaguely familiar; he'd seen just such a look in somebody's eyes. He felt cold, despite the heat under the trees where no cool breath of air could penetrate.

'Now what?' he asked.

'Now,' said Uncle Zeke, 'we turns.' He

studied the water for another moment, then veered his horse to the west, taking a course almost at right angles to the one they had been following.

'Good ground here,' he observed. 'Folks who know the Bottoms could build a road across 'em. But you gotta know 'em. Gotta know where the good ground is under the water, wherever there is water. We're all right now.'

He rode forward assuredly. Wayne kept beside him, but he was not free from apprehension. All the water looked too much alike to his inexperienced eye for comfort. Suppose Uncle Zeke made a mistake — well, it would be an unpleasant way to die.

However, Uncle Zeke evidently knew his business, for after half a mile or so sloshing through the treacherous film, the surface of the swamp sloped upward a little, the water ceased through natural drainage, and the horses found footing on comparatively firm soil.

Uncle Zeke reined in and pointed to the ground, which was scored by hoof marks.

'Fellers who drove those cows in here knowed the Bottoms,' he observed. 'Knowed just where to turn, after making tracks nobody could follow, not even a bloodhound. You figure to go ahead after 'em,

Mistuh Jim?'

'Yes,' Wayne replied. 'I want to learn where those cows went. You figure we'll be okay from here on?'

'Don't you worry,' answered the coloured man. 'Ol' Bottoms can't fool me. Let's go.'

'Suppose night catches us in here?'

'Don't you worry,' Uncle Zeke repeated. 'Plenty of good places to camp in the Bottoms, if you know where to look for 'em. I got cold fried chicken and cawn pone in my saddle pouches, and coffee and a little bucket. We'll make out.'

'Uncle Zeke, you're a wonder,' Wayne declared. 'You think of everything.' Uncle Zeke chuckled.

'Man and boy, I done lived a long time,' he said. 'You gotta learn to think of everything if you 'spect to keep on living.'

They rode on. The hoof-prints, deeply scored in the soft earth, were easy to follow, and Wayne experienced a growing exultation. His hunch had been a straight one, and if things worked out as he hoped they would, he would solve the mystery of the missing cattle and be in a position to give the wide-loopers their come-uppance. With no further qualms he jogged along beside the old coloured man, who kept shooting glances in every direction but never slowed

164

his pace.

Now it was growing quite gloomy under the trees, which were draped with long strings of sad-hued moss that gave them a ghostly appearance; and as darkness drew near, the hitherto deathly silent swamp awoke to vocal life. Frogs began croaking, and from the volume of sound they emitted, Wayne concluded that they must be giants of their species. Night birds uttered weird cries that blended unharmoniously with the sleepy chirping of daytime songsters who found refuge in the thickets. Sucking noises, perhaps caused by the sinking of areas of swamp or the bursting of gas bubbles, were heard from time to time. Altogether, it was an eerie chorus and hard on the nerves.

The growth thinned a little, and before them stretched a stream. It was about fifty yards in width, the colour of ink, its oily surface pierced by the snags of rotting stumps like crooked and reaching fingers, spotted with reeds and trailing vines. Little ripples showed where reptiles crossed and recrossed. It was a veritable Styx, flowing on slowly to the depths of the infernal regions.

'The Black Water,' Uncle Zeke observed sententiously as he turned his horse's head parallel with the stream.

'And that's what Cullen Barnet was supposed to go into, eh?' Wayne remarked. 'If he did, I don't see how he ever came out alive.'

'The Devil takes care of his own,' said Uncle Zeke. 'Tracks are running right along the creek. Got a notion all we have to do is follow the creek and we'll get to where they're headed, even when it gets too dark to see 'em. Yep, that's the Black Water, where the haunts go boat-riding, or so the swamp folks will tell you.'

'It looks it,' growled Wayne.

Suddenly the air quivered to a veritable devils' choir of horrific sound, a heart-rending cacophony, the wails of frightened children in distress, as if all the babies in the world were crying together. Its hideous mournfulness turned Wayne sick; his flesh crawled; he felt as if he had to clap his hands over his ears to shut out that agonized plea of helplessness and despair. Then, as abruptly as it had started, the awful serenade ceased.

'Good Lord! what was it?' Wayne asked.

' 'Gators,' Uncle Zeke returned composedly.

'Alligators?'

'Yep, big ones. They come up from the

river. Swamp 'gators always sing that way when it's getting dark and they're hungry. They'll follow us as we ride, hoping, with just their eyes showing, and now and then a snout when they take a little air; don't need much. You don't never want to walk close to the bank. Big tail flip out, wham! Into the water you go — 'gators' dinner.'

'No wonder folks think this devil-hole is haunted,' Wayne growled. 'I'm inclined to agree with them. There they go again!'

The wails broke forth with redoubled intensity. Uncle Zeke leaned far over in the saddle, plucked a sturdy dead branch from the ground and flung it into the water. There was a splashing, a raucous bellow like that of an angry bull stuck in the mud, a frightful howl, then silence.

'Now ol' 'gators are really mad,' chuckled Uncle Zeke. 'They thought that was something to eat. Some folks say they sing like that to make animals come into the water, where they can get 'em. I don't think so, but it could be.'

'Anything could be here,' Wayne retorted. 'If I was in here by myself, I'd climb the tallest tree I could find and stay there till it got light.'

Uncle Zeke chuckled. 'Ol' Bottoms sorta hard on folks till they get used to 'em,' he conceded. 'Guess we'd better be moving on and keep eyes open for a place to camp; soon be full dark.'

It was indeed very gloomy under the spreading branches of the moss-draped trees. Nearby the Black Water hissed against its black banks. Wayne could feel the eyes of the hopeful alligators.

They began rounding a bend and came face to face with a man mounted on a chestnut horse. Not twenty paces distant, he jerked his mount to a halt with a yelp of alarm. His hand flashed down.

CHAPTER SEVENTEEN

Wayne sent Flame surging in front of Uncle Zeke, hands streaking to his guns. Back and forth gushed the reddish flashes. The two riders were vague shadows, huge, grotesque, blasting death at each other through the murk; it was blind shooting. The guns boomed like thunder. The alligators wailed. Frightened birds squawked.

A slug ripped through Wayne's sleeve. Another caused him to gasp as it grazed his ribs. Just as he pulled trigger with both hands, the chestnut horse reared high. It gave an almost human scream, floundered sideways and fell into the creek. Its rider was flung from the hull like a stone from a sling and struck the water with a prodigious splash.

There was a raucous bellowing, another frightful howl, then scream on scream of agony and terror. The water was lashed to a bloody foam.

Gradually the awful tumult stilled, save for a crunching sound as big teeth cracked and splintered bones. Wayne sagged forward in his saddle, fighting a sickening nausea that rose in his throat. With fingers that trembled he reloaded his guns.

Uncle Zeke regarded the scene of horrible death philosophically. 'Guess ol' 'gators got their dinner,' he remarked.

Wayne snapped erect. 'Back away from here and into the brush,' he ordered. 'Could be some more of the hellions within hearing distance. Back out of sight and wait.'

In a nearby dense thicket, well concealed by the outer fringe of growth, they sat their horses, peering and listening. The alligators had finished their unexpected feast. The tumult in the Black Water had ceased, and of the unfortunate horse and its rider only a few splintered bones remained, starting on their long, long journey to the sea.

Aside from the croaking of frogs, the occasional cry of a night bird and the sinister hissing of the Black Water against its banks, the swamplands maintained their habitual dismal silence. Finally Wayne said:

'I think that hombre was by himself. And I also think that he came from the outfit's hideaway, and that it's not far off.'

'Got a notion you're right,' agreed Uncle

Zeke. 'S'pose we amble along and see.'

Wayne nodded, and they rode on very slowly; keeping a respectful distance from the ominous Black Water.

'Mistuh Jim,' Uncle Zeke suddenly said, 'I think we're following a trail, one that's been travelled quite a bit. I can't see anything, but I can feel it.'

'I think so, too,' Wayne replied. 'And I'm ready to bet a hatful of pesos that it is going to lead us to what I'm looking for. Take it easy, though; we might still run into something we won't like.'

Confident but cautious, they continued on their way. After an eighth of a mile or so of slow progress, Uncle Zeke sniffed loudly and said, 'I smell smoke.'

'I do, too,' Wayne answered. 'I've a notion we're getting close. Careful now; we mustn't take chances.'

A few more minutes, and abruptly the stand of trees and chaparral ended and before them lay a wide open space, clearly outlined in the bright starlight. And over to one side loomed the dark bulk of a good-sized cabin. From its stick-and-mud chimney rose a tiny trickle of smoke.

Nor was that all. More than half the cleared space was fenced to make a tight corral capable of holding several hundred head of cattle.

'This is it!' Wayne breathed exultantly as they drew rein and sat gazing at the scene spread before their eyes.

'Yep, this is it,' agreed Uncle Zeke. 'Looks like there ain't anybody home, either. Gotta be sure about that, though. Mighty bad snakes hang out in the Bottoms, and some of 'em got two legs.'

For some time they sat motionless, gazing at the cabin and its surroundings. The shack had a lonely and deserted look. Wayne studied it intently, but Uncle Zeke kept glancing around, his brows knitting.

'Mistuh Jim,' he whispered suddenly, 'I remember this clearin'. I saw it once before, long time back. Old cabin was there then — it was built by a trapping and hunting feller, Pappy told me. But back then there wasn't any corral; feller had a garden patch, Pappy said. Yep, I know right where I am now. Black Water runs in back of it, and I know a way out that's a better one than the way we come in. We're okay now. And there's a back door and a window to the shack which is built up close to the brush. We'll leave the horses here and sneak around back. Maybe we'll peek through the window and see if anbody's inside. Don't think there is, but we'll make sure.'

With the greatest caution they crept around the edge of the growth until they could approach the cabin from the rear. Edging forward, slow step by slow step, they peered through the smeared windowpanes. It was very shadowy inside, but gradually, by the faint glow from a bed of coals that smouldered in a big fireplace, they could see a table, chairs, and bunks built against the walls, and that they were unoccupied. Nowhere was there sight or sound of life.

'Nobody in there,' Wayne said. 'Let's have a look around.'

The back door opened easily, and they found themselves in the single room of the cabin.

'Guess we can risk a light,' Wayne decided. He struck a match and touched it to the wick of a bracket lamp. A mellow glow filled the cabin.

In a corner stood a dozen or so rifles, their parallel barrels gleaming like the pipes of an organ. There was a store of staple provisions on shelves pegged to the logs that formed the walls, a bucket of water and fuel stacked beside the fireplace. On the bunks were tumbled blankets.

'A hangout, all right,' Wayne observed.

'Yep,' agreed Uncle Zeke. 'Looks like folks have been holing up here for quite a spell;

173

it's a regular home. Now what we going to do with it?'

'Nothing, at present,' Wayne replied. For a moment he stood in thought.

'Uncle Zeke,' he said then, 'nothing was left of that hellion who went into the Black Water, or of his poor devil of a horse, either; nothing to cause the rest of the bunch to suspect that somebody has been here. Right?'

'That's right,' Uncle Zeke agreed.

'So when they have use for this place, they'll come back to it, feeling they're still secure here, as they have been in the past. We'll watch and wait, and perhaps we'll get a chance to land on them here and clean up the whole devilish outfit.'

'That's a notion, all right,' said Uncle Zeke. 'Wonder if ol' Cullen Barnet really is still alive and kickin'? Betcha this was his squattin' place, all right.'

'I wish I knew for sure,' Wayne replied. 'I'd feel easier if I was sure this is just a regulation brush-popping bunch of cow thieves and not an organization with a shrewd devil like Barnet at the head of it. Well, I think we'd better be getting out of here. Do you think you can find a place to camp for the night, where we dare light a fire? I could sure stand a cup of coffee, steaming hot, right now.'

'Yep, I can find a place; done told you I know where I'm at now,' said Uncle Zeke.

'Then let's go, on the chance some more of the bunch might happen along for some reason or other.'

Before leaving the cabin, Wayne made sure that no trace of their visit to it was left behind. He even picked up the stem of the match with which he had lit the lamp and cast it on the still glowing coals.

'Wonder what that hellion was doing here?' he remarked as he blew out the lamp and then carefully closed the door. 'Smells like he'd been cooking something.'

'Wouldn't be surprised if there's 'most always one of the scalawags here, to make sure nobody comes snoopin' around,' guessed Uncle Zeke.

'Could be,' Wayne conceded. 'Well, they'll wonder what became of him, but I figure they'll just decide he hightailed off somewhere. Really no reason for them to think otherwise. Let's go.'

Uncle Zeke was as good as his word. Riding west from the cabin, then turning south, he led the way to a stand of trees with thick growth between the trunks and tufts of grass the horses would find better than nothing. Nearby was a trickle of water.

Soon coffee was bubbling in a little flat bucket and a bountiful supply of fried chicken and corn pone was spread on a clean white cloth Uncle Zeke had thoughtfully provided.

It was cosy in the thicket, with ruddy gleams of the fire reflecting back from the cathedral arches of the branches overhead. The surrounding growth seemed to edge close in a friendly fashion, moving nearer the warm glow. The world and its cares, its anxieties, its apprehensions and its uncertainties seemed to be shut out, warded off by the soft blanket of silence that swathed the swamplands.

'Different here from what we passed through a while back,' Wayne remarked. 'Makes a person feel content, free from worry, just satisfied to drift along.'

The eyes of shrewd old Uncle Zeke twinkled.

'Beginning to get you, eh, Mistuh Jim? Be careful. Don't play footsie with the swamplands. First thing you know they'll reach out and gather you in, claim you for their own. Careful how you drink swamp water. Looks plumb harmless, but it ain't. Once down inside you, it's liable to whisper, "Ain't ever had no water like this, eh, man? Makes you feel warm and comfy, eh? Makes you wanta come back and get more." And up in the treetops you'll hear a little chuckle, sorta like a chipmunk talking to himself. Only he ain't talking to himself. He's talking to *you*. Watch out you don't listen too close. 'Cause if you do, you'll hear that little chucklin' voice when you're way far off. And first thing you know you'll be heading back to the swamplands. And lots of folks who have done that, they've come back to stay.'

'I can well believe it.' Wayne sighed. Suddenly he cocked his head in an attitude of listening, looked up. Then, meeting the twinkle in Uncle Zeke's eyes, he grinned sheepishly.

'I think we'd better eat,' he said. Uncle Zeke chuckled, and poured steaming coffee.

CHAPTER EIGHTEEN

They were astir at daybreak. While Wayne cared for the horses, Uncle Zeke boiled a pot of coffee, which they drank.

'Guess this and wind pudding will have to hold us till we get back to the ranch,' he observed. 'You all finished down here, Mis-tuh Jim?'

'Yes,' Wayne replied. 'I've learned what I wanted to learn. Now all we can do is to sit tight and wait for an opportunity to put the knowledge to use. How or when I haven't the slightest idea.'

'Something will work out; always does,' said Uncle Zeke. 'Now I'll show you another way out of the Bottoms, an easier way than the one we came in by.'

It was indeed a much better route than the watery one by which they had entered the swamps — a faint trail that seemed on the verge of losing itself in the thickets or other stands of growth but always provided a feasible way of passage.

'Wouldn't be surprised if ol' Cullen used this one when he was here,' remarked Uncle Zeke. 'Wouldn't use it to run cows in, though; they'd leave tracks.'

As they rode, Wayne carefully memorized everything that could be construed as a landmark. Uncle Zeke noted this and smiled.

'Think you could find your way back in, Mistuh Jim?' he asked.

'Yes, I think I could,' Wayne replied. 'Like most plainsmen, I have a pretty good instinct for distance and direction, and with a few guide-posts, such as I've noted, I believe I could make it back in alone, if I should happen to need to.'

'Hope you won't,' said Uncle Zeke. 'You'd be better off with somebody along who knows the Bottoms.'

'I won't argue that,' Wayne conceded, 'but you never can tell how things may work out. So I'm doing my best to prepare against just such an eventuality.'

Finally they reached the edge of the swamplands; the open prairie shimmered in the sun. Before passing from the final fringe of growth, Wayne carefully scanned their surroundings against the possibility of some chance watcher. However, the rangeland stretched lonely and deserted on all sides. They rode out and turned north, arriving at the JH ranch house in the middle of the afternoon. There they found Ward Handley, the range boss, in a decidedly perturbed frame of mind.

'Where the devil you been?' he demanded. 'I was beginning to think you'd flown the coop.'

Wayne told him, after first cautioning him to keep what he learned under his hat. Handley shook his head and swore.

'You're getting to be a darn good cattleland detective,' he commented. 'Next thing you know the Rangers will be making a bid for you.'

'I doubt it.' Wayne smiled. 'But anyhow, we now know where the bunch hangs out, and where they hole up stolen cows while awaiting a favourable opportunity to run them east or west. Which is something.'

'You're darn right it's something,' Handley agreed. 'I predict we'll make a clean sweep of the hellions the next time we tangle with them. Say, tying on to Uncle Zeke was one of the best things you ever did.'

Wayne thought so, too, and reflected on the importance of seemingly inconsequential happenings. He had offered the old col-

180

oured man a job out of gratitude for his help in frustrating the attempt to delay the right-of-way grading, never thinking that Uncle Zeke might well be the deciding factor in his war with the rustlers.

Well satisfied with the results of his expedition into the Big Bottoms, Wayne decided that he had earned a little diversion. He bathed, shaved, dressed with care and rode west by slightly north, arriving at the Tumbling D ranch house just at sunset.

Old Watson Ray, seated on the veranda, let out a whoop of welcome.

'How are you, son?' he cried. 'Plumb glad to see you. Come in! Come in! Gyp, look who's here!'

Gypsy appeared in the doorway, her eyes bright. Together they entered the *casa,* after a wrangler had taken charge of Flame.

'Just in time to eat,' said Ray. 'And this time you're going to spend the night if I have to hogtie you.'

'Be glad to,' Wayne accepted, looking hard at Gypsy, who smiled and blushed.

'Fine!' said Ray. 'Gyp, put him in the big room at the head of the stairs — show him which one.'

They ascended the stairs together. Gypsy opened a door to reveal a neatly furnished room with two windows.

'Our guest room,' she said. 'I hope you'll find it comfortable. Grandpa's is in the back. The cook sleeps downstairs, off the kitchen. There's nobody else in the house at present.'

'Your range boss was over yesterday evening, making roundup arrangements,' Ray remarked as they waited for the cook to beller. 'Understand they aim to hold it on the Boxed E east pasture, across from your spread.'

'Yes, that's about the most central location for the main holding spot,' Wayne replied.

'I don't think my cows have strayed much yet, but I'll have two or three of my boys there to lend a hand on the chance some have drifted,' Ray promised.

After supper, he and Wayne discussed range matters and the coming roundup for some time. Finally old Watson lumbered upstairs to bed.

'See you in the morning,' he said. 'Get a good night's rest.'

In the living-room, Gypsy adroitly led the conversation until she had her guest talking about himself. Before he realized it, he was telling her everything: his plans, his hopes, his ambitions. She listened intently, without interrupting.

'I think,' she said when he paused, 'that you are going to enjoy great success.'

'Yes,' he replied. 'I'll enjoy it when and if it comes, if I have the right person to enjoy it with me.'

She did not pretend not to understand, and the blue eyes met his honestly.

'This makes only the second time you've seen me,' she pointed out.

'The first time was enough,' he answered. 'I mean it.'

'Yes, I think you do,' she said slowly.

'And you?'

Again the honest meeting of eyes. 'What's the sense in being coy?' she said. 'In this country life is uncertain. No telling what will happen from one day to the next. There may well be no tomorrow. So why not make the most of what we have?'

Another instant, and she was in his arms.

After Wayne headed for home the following morning, old Watson asked:

'Well, honey, now how do you like him?'

For no apparent good reason, the innocent question caused her to blush hotly.

'Plenty,' she said. Old Watson chuckled.

'Got a notion I'm liable to lose my gal,' he said playfully.

'Well, wouldn't you rather lose her to your next door neighbour, within easy riding distance, than to somebody way off?' she retorted.

'Guess I would,' he admitted. Suddenly he looked startled.

'Say!' he exclaimed. 'You trying to tell me you're going to marry that young feller?'

'Of course,' she answered. 'I made up my mind about that the first time I laid eyes on him. Only he didn't know it then.'

Old Watson threw out his hands and groaned.

'What chance does a poor man have?' he lamented.

'None at all,' his granddaughter replied composedly. 'Are you just finding that out?'

When Wayne reached the JH ranch house, he found Handley getting ready to ride out on to the range.

'Everything okay?' the range boss asked. 'How's the little gal?'

'She's fine,' Wayne replied. 'She'll be moving in with us soon after the roundup.'

Handley's jaw dropped. 'Say!' he sputtered. 'You work fast!' He grinned broadly.

'Fine!' he chortled. 'Just what you need: a nice wife to hold you steady. And she'll make a nice one. Purty as a spotted dog under a red wagon. She's got everything!'

'You're telling me!' Wayne replied with emphasis.

After caring for his horse, Jim Wayne sat down in his living-room to smoke and try to think. His mind was in a considerable turmoil, and his thoughts whirled around like birds in a cage or a squirrel on a wheel, going places but getting exactly nowhere.

Altogether, he was in the normal condition of a young man very much in love. Finally he gave up any attempt at coherent thought and went out to the kitchen to chat with Uncle Zeke, who was alone at the moment, the cook having driven to town to replenish supplies.

Uncle Zeke was delighted when Wayne told him his intentions. The humour wrinkles around his eyes deepened and his black face seemed to become one great grin.

'Fine!' he chuckled. 'I'm sure glad for you, Mistuh Jim. Getting married is mighty fine for a man. I was married for thirty years, till the Good Lord figured He had work for her to do some place else, and I know. If things are going good, she's glad with you, and if they ain't just what they ought to be, it's mighty comfortin' to feel her hand on yours in a dark hour and know that she's with you, good or bad, and always will be. And when you get old, and maybe are alone, it's mighty fine to look back on such things and to know that though she's gone away for a while, she's still with you and always will be. The Scriptures say it ain't good for a man to live alone, and the Scriptures are always right. Yes, Mistuh Jim, I'm mighty glad for you. Bless you both!'

Jim Wayne bowed his head.

A little later he went out into the sunshine. His mind was again clear, filled with a quiet happiness. He felt uplifted by Uncle Zeke's simple homily, and he agreed with every word of it. Yes, the fruits of ambition would be the sweeter were there someone with whom to share them.

But it was time he climbed down from his rosy-hued cloud and turned his attention to more prosaic matters. The roundup was only a couple of days off, and that meant work for everybody, including himself. He got the rig on the big bay, Flame having earned a rest, and rode on a tour of inspection. It was well past dark when he returned to the ranch house, well satisfied with the way things were going.

The following evening he paid a hurried visit to the Tumbling D spread, having an important matter to discuss with Watson Ray. He approached the *casa* with some trepidation.

'Let me soften him up a bit first,' Gypsy had warned before Wayne had headed for home on the occasion of his former visit. 'He thinks I'm still only nine years old.'

However, old Watson greeted him warmly. 'Yep, you can have her,' he said without preamble. 'I figure she could do a devil of a sight worse. Was always scared she'd marry a cowhand and have to live in a clapboard shack.'

'I wouldn't mind — with Jim,' Gypsy said blithely.

'Mighty cold in winter,' her grandfather pointed out.

'Oh, we'd keep warm,' she answered confidently.

'I don't doubt it,' old Watson returned dryly. 'You haven't got that red in your hair for nothing.'

'And that,' said Gypsy, her colour rising, 'will be about enough of that.'

CHAPTER NINETEEN

Roundup days! Dust and sun and sweat and blood. The acrid stench of scorched hair and the pungent whiff of wood smoke. The bawling of cattle and the shouting of men. Bitter toil throughout the long, hot days. Laughter and jollity and good fellowship around the campfire at night.

At a meeting held by the various owners, Jim Wayne, now thoroughly familiar with the section, had been elected roundup boss. His word was law in all matters pertaining to the roundup, with no one to gainsay him. The same would have obtained if, instead of being an owner, he hadn't owned a hoof. The owners were as much under his jurisdiction as were the cowboys. Until the last cow was driven back to its home range or to the loading pens, the roundup boss's word was law.

Wayne's first chore was to select as many chief helpers as he thought necessary;

188

competent, experienced riders of good judgment who could be relied upon not only for the routine activities of the roundup, but for possible emergency.

These trusted subordinates would be put in command of groups of punchers that were to comb the range thoroughly in search of groups of cattle and lone-wolf old mossy-horns as well. Wayne had already worked out a plan by which the broad reaches of the wild terrain could be worked to produce the most satisfactory results. He assembled his men and told them:

'I don't want any strays in thickets or gulches after this roundup is over. That will mean bad combing. Each of you is responsible for the ground he covers, and if it isn't covered properly, somebody will answer to me personally.'

After a good look at the speaker, and recalling his reputation, the hands decided emphatically that there would be no bad combing.

Away went the troop of cowboys, racing their horses and whooping, the various groups flying off in different directions like the fragments from an exploding shell.

Once well away from the holding spot and the assembled chuck wagons, they slowed their pace and got down to business. Soon the groups scattered, until the men were separated by distances that varied according to the topography of the terrain. It was each man's chore to hunt out all the cattle on the range over which he rode. When it was rough and broken, with gullies and thickets, the chore was not an easy one. And careful combing was necessary. Sometimes small groups were rooted out. Then again obstreperous individuals had to be flushed from their hiding-places, to the accompaniment of ruffled tempers and vivid profanity, some hands insisting that cuss words were the only language the blankety-blank-blank ornery hellions could understand.

After the rider had collected all the cows he could handle, the number depending on the age and temperament of the critters in question, he drove his irritated charges to the designated holding spot or parade grounds.

The cowboys surrounded the captured cattle and held them in close herd, a compact group from which individuals were not allowed to stray.

When the roundup boss decided enough cows had been concentrated, the next chore was the cutting out. Meanwhile the cooks had been busy and the noonday meal was ready.

'We'll eat before we sift 'em,' Wayne said.

After the meal was finished, the cowboys smoked cigarettes, yawned, stretched and mounted fresh horses, and the cutting out began.

Cutting out was no chore for the amateur. It called for bold and skilful horsemanship and was fraught with not little danger for horse and man, the needle-point horns and splaying hoofs of an enraged cow being something to reckon with. Trained, nimble-footed horses were used for the work.

The brand of the cow a calf was following was carefully noted. The little fellow was roped and dragged to the fire where the various branding irons were heated. The calf was flipped over on its side, the proper iron snaked out of the fire and applied. There was a sizzling sound, the stench of burned hair, a bawl from the calf. If the calf in question happened to be a bull yearling, there was the flash of a knife and another necessary operation was performed to the accompaniment of a louder bawl. The brand was called; the tally man repeated it and wrote it down. The animal was released and very quickly was contentedly grazing, its troubles forgotten.

All very simple, most of the time, but not always.

The various brands were driven to the proper subsidiary holding spots, a spot being allotted to each ranch represented.

The cows wanted for shipping were segregated in the beef cut, the others allowed to drift back to their feeding grounds after they had been driven on to their home range.

Just the routine chores of the longhorn empire, all in the day's work. And if a horse fell while zigzagging through the milling herd and its unfortunate rider was torn and broken under churning hoofs, that too was all in the day's work.

And just such a tragedy threatened the Fort Worth country roundup.

It was on the second day of the roundup. An angry cow, whose calf had just been released and was bawling and wailing, rushed at a young puncher, who laughingly wheeled his horse to dodge the wrathful bovine. His mount's irons skated on a patch of grass that had been beaten down to a smooth and slick surface but not yet ground to dust. The cayuse stumbled, lost its footing and fell. The cowboy was hurled from the saddle to strike the ground with stunning force, directly in the path of the cow, which gave a bellow of triumph and charged, horns lowered.

Men yelled with consternation; there was

a mad grab for guns. Jim Wayne, who was less than a score of yards distant, sent Flame racing parallel with the cow. He left the saddle in a streaking dive. His left hand shot across the cow's neck, gripping the tip of the left horn, and his right seized the base of the right horn. He hurled his long body sideways. A wrenching twist and the cow went down, striking the ground with a crash, all the breath and most of the fight knocked out of her. The animal was almost on top of the fallen cowboy, who was struggling to rise.

A cheer went up. A dozen riders surged forward. The cow was roped, the other cattle fended off. The fallen hand got to his feet and limped away from danger.

'Much obliged, Jim,' he said over his shoulder. 'All in a day's work.'

Finally the roundup was over. The tally was carefully checked. And there was the devil to pay! Every outfit except the JH and the recently arrived Tumbling D had lost cows, or so their owners maintained. Ran Ellis set his Boxed E losses at two hundred, at least.

'Looks like the hellions got more than the hundred I told you about,' he said to Wayne. 'What the devil are we going to do?'

'*We've* got to organize and stamp it out,'

Wayne replied. 'This can't be allowed to go on.'

The owners met to discuss the matter. Jim Wayne was given the floor.

'Gentlemen,' he said, 'undoubtedly we are up against a criminal organization headed by somebody with brains.'

'Who the devil could it be?' somebody demanded.

'I expect,' answered Wayne, 'that we'll be mightily surprised when we learn who. Consider the Fabens McCord outfit. They terrorized three counties, and in their trail they left dozens of murders — you can read of their depredations in the files of court proceedings. Fabens McCord himself maintained a front of respectability. He lived in a fine big ranch house, dressed well, appeared educated, courteous, generous. He was highly regarded by upright businessmen with whom he associated. Meanwhile he suborned law enforcement officers, handing out a thousand dollars here and there where it would do the most good. He was the brains and the front. And behind the front his hellions operated brazenly. They widelooped cows without number, saw to it that honest sheriffs or other law enforcement officers met with "accidents". Finally decent people had enough of it. They got together under the leadership of a nice old gentleman, Mr. Charles Grantham.

' "You fellers have all got guns," ' said Mr. Grantham. "You know that Fabens McCord is at the head of the hellions. All right. Bring in every McCord devil you can catch alive. Shoot first and don't ask questions. Don't leave any except the dead ones." '

A chuckle ran through the gathering. Wayne grinned, and resumed:

'The decent citizens did just that. Ultimately, they brought in six alive, all that was left of the McCord bunch. Mr. Grantham held court. Previously he had prevailed on the Governor to appoint him judge to replace a certain slippery individual who had hastily "resigned". Mr. Grantham saw to it that the defendants got a fair trial. After that he superintended the hanging of all six, including Fabens McCord. Yes, most people were greatly surprised when Fabens McCord was exposed. Such things have happened before, quite a few times. And folks hereabouts are liable to be quite surprised when we drop a loop on the brains of the outfit.'

'Any notion who he is, Jim?' asked Ellis.

'Not the slightest,' Wayne replied, adding grimly, 'but I intend to find out.'

'He'll do it,' chuckled an old rancher. 'No

doubt in my mind as to that. So, boys, if you learn anything, get it to Jim without wasting a minute.'

The beef cuts headed for Fort Worth, where a number of buyers were assembled to bid for the stock. Wayne, however, drove his cows straight to the stockyards, as per agreement with the packing house people, where they were immediately accepted and paid for.

Wayne received payment by cheque, but the buyers, in the traditional cow country custom, paid cash, most of which was deposited in the Fort Worth bank.

Leaving the stockyards, Wayne made his way to the Western Star saloon for a confab with Sweatless Sam. As he drew near the entrance he saw Malcolm Otey come out. Otey waved a greeting and mounted a tall dark bay horse hitched to a nearby rack. He turned the cayuse and rode west at a swift pace. Wayne idly watched his departure.

Suddenly he stared, leaning forward as if to peer closer. His amazed, incredulous expression changed slowly to one of stark certainty.

Malcolm Otey sat his horse like a centaur, head up, back straight, shoulders squared, swaying gracefully to the movement of his mount.

Wayne continued to gaze until Otey turned a corner. He straightened up and passed a hand across his eyes, as if doubting his own vision.

'I didn't see his face, but I knew I'd never forget the way he rode!' he muttered aloud. He pushed through the swinging doors and headed straight for the bar. He felt the need of a drink, two drinks, maybe three, for he was stunned by what he had learned. There was not the slightest doubt in his mind but that Malcolm Otey was the man he chased into the Big Bottoms the night of the attempted wide-looping of the JH herd.

CHAPTER TWENTY

He downed his first drink at a gulp, toyed with the second, endeavouring to correlate his thoughts and properly evaluate what he had learned. Carefully he reviewed his contacts with Otey. They had been few but significant. From the very first he had sensed a hostility on the real estate man's part.

Now — marvel of perspicacity — he told himself sarcastically, he could see that Otey wove in and out of the various activities like a shadowy evil spirit transplanted from the age of the Medicis. He was indeed a shadow, never obtrusive but always working shrewdly and skilfully in the background. The first time he had seen Otey, he had catalogued him as an able and adroit man. He was in fact too able and adroit, viciously cunning, with a sadistic streak of cruelty.

Otey had ridden north with the trail herds, presumably bound for Dodge City and business affairs, the nature of which he did not divulge. There followed the wide-looping of a herd of Lafe Swanson's cattle the night of the storm, and the murder of one of his hands. At the time Wayne had been convinced that a bunch from around Fort Worth was responsible. Then came the attempt to rustle another herd north of the Cimarron which he, Wayne, had frustrated, after which there was proof that it had indeed been a Fort Worth outfit which had made the try.

In Dodge City he had contacted Otey, and shortly afterwards had come the abortive endeavour to kill him. And Otey had left town early the following morning in a nervous and irritable frame of mind, according to the hotel desk clerk, breaking his two o'clock appointment with Wayne, possibly because he was perturbed over the failure of his murder plot and not sure just how much his intended victim had learned or guessed. The three men who had died in the course of the ruckus had been identified by the town marshal as Texans, and it was logical to believe that they were members of the wide-looping outfit.

Wayne had been inclined to think at the time that the attempt on his life was in retaliation for his frustration of the rustling attempt on the Cimarron. But, since Otey was now alarmed, it could have been for the purpose of eliminating him as a possible menace to his nefarious activities.

Then had come the brush with the grade patrol by the outlaws, with the destruction of the all-important locomotive in mind. Otey had bitterly opposed the coming of the railroad to Fort Worth and well knew that disabling the engine would result in a fatal delay that would prevent the tracks from reaching Fort Worth before the land grant subsidy expired.

Yes, he had made out a very good case against the hellion, but, unfortunately, one that wouldn't stand up in court. It was pure conjecture on his part.

Well, he had an ace in the hole, thanks to Uncle Zeke: he knew where the devils hung out. Now all he had to do was corral them there. Considerable of a chore, everything considered, but perhaps he'd get a lucky break.

With a shrug of his broad shoulders he dismissed the whole matter for the moment as Sweatless Sam lumbered over to greet him.

'Looks like the making of a wild night,' observed Sweatless. 'S'pose we sit down for a while. Liable to be the last chance I'll get

200

between now and daylight.'

'A good notion; I haven't eaten yet,' Wayne agreed to the suggestion.

They sat down at a corner table; Sweatless beckoned to a waiter and Wayne gave his order.

'The boys are mighty pleased with the stock you delivered,' Sweatless remarked. 'As fine a bunch of beef as they ever laid eyes on. They decided they could use quite a few more cows — business is booming — and sent word to Ran Ellis to bring along what he's got.'

'Glad to hear it,' Wayne replied. 'He's okay.'

'So everybody thinks, after you took up with him,' agreed Sweatless. 'Folks say he must be all right or you wouldn't have done it; they don't look sideways at him any more. You did him good in more ways than one. Since you handed him that walloping he's simmered down quite a bit. Learned there are better men in the world than him.'

Wayne laughed and didn't argue the point. He believed that Ellis's former truculence had been based on resentment against what he considered an unjustified attitude on the part of his neighbours. When that attitude was replaced by one of friendliness, he quickly cooled off and was ready to meet others more than half-way.

The Western Star was really filling up now, and growing livelier by the minute. The cowboys, money in their pockets, were out for a royal bust, no holds barred. A crowd of railroad builders added to the tumult. The roulette wheels spun so fast they smoked. The dance floor was crowded, with barely room enough for couples to shuffle.

Some of the perspiring bartenders had given up taking time to pull corks. They deftly knocked the necks off bottles and gushed straight whisky over the splinters.

Ran Ellis pushed through the swinging door, searched the room with his eyes and spotted Wayne and Sweatless. He worked his way through the jam to their table.

'Much obliged,' he said without preamble.

'For what?' Wayne asked.

'You know what,' the Boxed E owner replied. 'I know you put in a word for me with the packing house people; they took my whole cut. With no shipping charges to pay, I'm better'n breaking even after my losses of the summer. You sure did me a good turn.'

'I just mentioned that your stock was above average,' Wayne said. Ellis chuckled and sat down.

'Uh-huh, that was all. You just sorta

intimated that you'd like it if they did business with me, and folks in this pueblo are mighty glad of a chance to do you a favour. There's quite a bit of talk about running you for Mayor.'

'It can stop at talk,' Wayne said emphatically. 'I've got enough on my hands running a spread and bucking wide-loopers without getting mixed up in a political brannigan. Besides, I'm not a citizen of Fort Worth; I live beyond the town limits.'

'Oh, don't let that bother you,' Ellis replied cheerfully. 'Fort Worth claims everything between here and New Mexico and is ready to back it up. I've a notion they'd stretch a point if you lived on the other side of the state line. Say! things are hoppin', ain't they? And it's this way all over town. Understand the railroaders got paid today, too.'

'Yep, this is their pay day,' said Sweatless. 'And they sure throw it to the winds. Good for business, but hard on the nervous system. If we don't have a ruckus or two before the night is out, I miss my guess.'

Wayne's dinner arrived. 'Sorry you had to wait so long, Mr. Wayne, but we're a mite rushed in the kitchen,' the waiter apologized.

'Don't let it bother you,' Wayne told him.

'I've got all night.' The waiter grinned and bobbed.

'And I'll have the same,' said Ellis, glancing at the dishes before Wayne.

'And I'm getting out of here,' growled Sweatless. 'Watching you young hellions eat makes me hungry, too. And with my waistline!'

'He's got one, all right, but he's sure quick on his feet for such a big jigger,' Ellis remarked as the saloon-keeper moved away. 'And he's darned good at handling trouble when it busts loose. I've a notion he may need to be good before the night is over; things sure are booming. With nearly all the hands in this section here and raising old Harry, it's bad enough. But just to whoop it up a bit more, a big trail herd has rolled in from the Devil's River country and aims to ship from here. They'll fill the stockyards as soon as our critters are out of the way. Every siding's lined with cow cars, and I heard the railroad is rushing more from the East. Yep, this section is beginning to catch on. Understand that Devil's River herd had originally planned to make the Dodge City drive, but changed their mind just before they started out. So Fort Worth gets the business. Those Devil's River riders are a salty-looking bunch. They'll make things lively. The town marshal has swore in a lot of special deputies and has one stationed in each saloon. He figures that if real trouble starts it'll be in the bars. Sheriff's keeping an eye on 'em, too.'

Wayne listened rather absently as Ellis chattered on, for his thoughts were elsewhere. The roundup was over, and within a few days he and Gypsy Ray would be married, which was enough to make any young man somewhat distrait.

However, it did not affect his appetite, and he put away a hefty surrounding without too much difficulty. Afterwards, over coffee and a cigarette, he surveyed the colourful scene with interest and quickly found himself absorbing the atmosphere of general gaiety.

Although it was but a little past ten o'clock, the Western Star was already roaring. The din was deafening, the air blue with smoke, rank with the stench of spilled whisky. Wayne decided he'd had all he could take. He was too preoccupied to be in a mood for drinking. Ellis and most of the hands were dancing or in card games. Sweatless Sam was circulating, trying to keep order or a semblance of it. A walk in the night air would help. He left the saloon and strolled along the street, turned on to a somewhat quieter side street.

Suddenly from directly ahead came wild shouting. Instinctively, his hands dropped towards the butts of his guns. Under a street light materialized three men. One, whose face and grizzled hair was streaked with blood, was being supported by the other two as he shambled along the street.

Wayne hurried forward. 'What's going on?' he demanded. 'What happened to him?'

He was recognized by one of the uninjured men. 'Hello, Mr. Wayne? It's Caleb, the night watchman at the bank. They pistol-whipped him and knocked him out. Busted open the bank and cleaned it. Must have gotten fifty thousand or better — big deposits today.'

CHAPTER
TWENTY-ONE

For an instant Jim Wayne was bereft of speech. Then he asked:

'Did you get a look at them, Caleb?'

'About all I saw was stars,' growled the watchman. 'I got just a glimpse of the hellions before they belted me and knocked me cold. There were three of 'em. One was big and tall, the other two sorta short. That's all I saw; they had handkerchiefs tied over their faces. Were waiting for me when I stepped around the corner.'

'We're taking him to the doctor,' one of the men interpolated.

'Go ahead; don't delay,' Wayne said. 'I'll have a look at the bank.'

When he reached the building, which was less than a block distant, the front door stood open and men were passing in and out. Quite likely the robbers had taken their departure by way of it. Wayne pushed his way through the excited crowd and took a look.

The vault door stood open. The combination knob had been neatly drilled out. The drill lay on the floor amid scattered papers and silver coin. Wayne turned and hurried out; nothing he could do there.

'Otey and what's left of his bunch, sure as blazes,' he muttered. 'And I'm just about sure for certain, now, that he really is Cullen Barnet who, it was said, could break open any safe in the country; that bank vault was not exactly a push-over. Cullen Barnet!'

Yes, Malcolm Otey was Cullen Barnet, a mad genius who had turned his back on the light; a prototype of John Ringo, Doc Holiday, Joe Hill and other cultured, intelligent men of great ability who for some reason had chosen the wrong fork of the trail.

What to do? He had a very good notion where the trio would head. Should he get a posse together, notify the sheriff and hightail after them? Wayne shook his head and quickened his pace. It would take time, and time was precious. He experienced a growing conviction that Otey was going to pull out. Why shouldn't he, with the big haul he'd just made? Fifty thousand dollars! Three of them, the watchman had said. Heavy odds to buck, but he believed the only chance to recover the money and bring the robbers to justice would be for him to go it alone. The robbers had a start, but Flame's great speed and endurance would cut down the lead. Maybe he could make it to the cabin in the Big Bottoms clearing in time. After he got there he'd try and figure something. They didn't have too much of a start. The blood on the watchman's face had hardly begun to congeal, which meant he hadn't been unconscious for a great length of time.

Leaving the main street, Wayne hastened to the stable where Flame was kept. He got the rig on the big sorrel, made sure his Winchester was smooth in the boot, and rode out of town by way of almost deserted side streets. From the uproar in the business section he knew word of the bank robbery had gotten around.

Wayne did not push his horse at first but allowed him gradually to build up speed; he had a long way to go. He felt sure that the cunning Otey would gain the clearing by way of the watery trail used by the stolen cattle, where no trace of his passing would be left. He, Wayne, had no intention of following that hazardous route. The one he chose would be longer but safer.

A nearly full moon was half-way up the

eastern slant of the sky, flooding the prairies with liquid silver. Quite distant objects were clearly visible. Wayne was convinced he could follow the furtive trail that led from the western terminal of the swamplands to the clearing, even by moonlight. If he made a mistake and lost the trail, he hoped Gypsy wouldn't grieve too much.

Mile after mile flowed past beneath the sorrel's drumming hoofs. The moon climbed higher, and before her chaste majesty the stars paled their ineffectual fires. Groves and thickets stood out in bold relief. Clumps of grazing cattle raised inquiring heads as the lone horseman thundered past. He reached the state lands to the south, rode parallel to the dark shadow that was the Bottoms, rounded their western edge and turned almost due south, straining his eyes to peer ahead.

Finally he sighted what he sought: two tall trees that stood as portals to the opening in the growth which marked the beginning of the trail. A few more minutes and he was swallowed by the ominous gloom of the swamplands.

The windings of the trail made it difficult to judge distance. With startling abruptness he reached the clearing. One moment he was riding between thick growth; the next the open space, shimmering with moonlight, was before him. He jerked Flame to a halt and sat gazing across to the far wall of growth. There, shouldering the chaparral, was the cabin. A single window glowed golden. Near the cabin was a lean-to; under it three saddled and bridled horses.

'They're in there, feller,' he muttered to Flame. 'Yes, all three of them, and all set to pull out soon. Okay, you'll have to hole up here while I try to slide around the edge of the brush to the back, like Uncle Zeke and I did. And for Pete's sake, don't go singing any songs to the moon!'

Confident that Flame, usually a very silent horse, would remain quiet, he forced him into the growth a little way and dropped the split reins to the ground. Then, with the greatest caution and very slowly, he stole along in the shadow of the growth and, after many a pause to peer and listen, reached the back of the cabin. The door stood slightly ajar, and through it came a rumble of voices. He edged to the window and got a view of the single room.

Seated at the table were three men. Two were stocky, hard-case individuals of evil countenance. The third was handsome, gentlemanly Malcolm Otey. On the table were three heaps of bills and gold coin; the canvas sacks in which the money had been stored lay on the floor.

Otey was speaking, in his musical, drawling voice, and the words came clearly to Wayne's ears.

'A little better than twenty thousand for each of us,' he said, a thin, cynical smile touching his lips as his gaze rested on his companions, who were staring greedily at the stacks of money. 'Yes, sixty-three thousand and a few odd hundreds altogether. Enough to put one man on easy street for a long time. We'll have a drink on it and then hightail; section's getting a mite hot since that blasted Wayne showed up, and we'll be better off elsewhere for a while.'

The others chuckled evilly and nodded agreement. Otey rose to his feet, turned to a nearby shelf. Wayne's hands gripped his gun-butts, then relaxed. Better to wait until the unsavoury trio were absorbed in their drinks; he should be able to slide through the door and get the drop on them. He knew he was taking a frightful risk but couldn't figure any safer way to do it.

From the shelf Otey took a bottle and three glasses. He shot a glance over his shoulder at the others, who had eyes for nothing but the fortune in gold and greenbacks on the table. His hand brushed over the tops of two of the glasses. Wayne wondered what he was doing. Then he filled the glasses to the brim, placed two on the table before his companions, held the third in his hand, and remained standing.

'Here's to more of the same kind,' he said, and raised his glass.

The others chortled, also raising their drinks and downing them at a gulp. Malcolm Otey's eyes glittered. He leaned forward a little, glass to lip, gazing expectantly.

Suddenly one of the seated pair stiffened in his chair. His eyes widened, bulged. His mouth opened, and from it came a frightful cry. He surged to his feet, reeled sideways and fell, writhing in agony.

Before his awful contortions had ceased the second man was also on his feet. He doubled over with an animal-like howl, gripping his middle. He tried to straighten and could not, screamed again and pitched forward on his face. He writhed for a moment, then, like his companion, was still. Malcolm Otey raised his glass and drained it, wiped his lips with the back of his hand, tossed the empty glass aside, smiled and began gathering up the money on the table. 'Enough to put *one* man on easy street!'

Sick, shaking, Jim Wayne leaned against the building wall. Too late he realized the significance of that hand movement across the glass tops. He drew his right-hand gun, half raised it. He knew he should shoot the sadistic killer where he stood, but he could not. His blood wasn't cold enough for that. He took a long stride and hit the sagging door with his shoulder, sending it wide open with a crash.

Malcolm Otey whirled at the sound and looked into the rock-steady muzzle of a levelled Colt. Wayne's voice blared at him:

'Elevate!'

His contorted features a mask of rage and hatred, Otey slowly raised his hands shoulder high.

Wayne half lowered his gun, started to take a step forward. Otey's right hand darted forward like the head of a striking snake. A stubby little double-barrelled derringer shot from his sleeve and spatted against his palm. The gambler's draw!

The unexpected move almost caught Wayne off balance — almost but not quite. The two guns boomed as one.

Wayne reeled sideways, blood pouring down his face, shooting as fast as he could pull the trigger.

Otey screamed as the slugs hammered into his body. He staggered back and leaped from the floor, grasping at the air as though seeking to clutch his own departing soul, and fell with a crash — dead.

Jim Wayne automatically holstered his gun and wiped away some of the blood that flowed from a bullet cut just above his left temple. He stared woodenly at the bodies on the floor.

'Another notch for my gun-stock,' he muttered. 'Pray God it'll be the last.'

Wearily he gathered up the money and stowed it in the sacks. He could not bring himself to touch the bodies. Let the sheriff ride down and do with them whatever he saw fit. On feet that seemed numb and legs without feeling, he walked out of the cabin and whistled to Flame. In a moment the sorrel paced across the clearing, snorting inquiringly. Wayne stowed the canvas sacks in his saddle pouches. Then he got the rigs off the three horses under the lean-to and left them to fend for themselves, which they could do till the sheriff picked them up. Without a backward glance at the cabin of death, he mounted. When he reached the open prairie, he did not head for home. Instead, he rode a long diagonal north by west that would take him to the Tumbling D ranch house.

After the night of horror he wanted Gypsy as he'd never wanted her before; wanted her understanding, the comfort of her voice, her hand on his. . . .

ABOUT THE AUTHOR

Leslie Scott was born in Lewisburg, West Virginia. During the Great War, he joined the French Foreign Legion and spent four years in the trenches. In the 1920s he worked as a mining engineer and bridge builder in the western American states and in China before settling in New York. A bar-room discussion in 1934 with Leo Margulies, who was managing editor for Standard Magazines, prompted Scott to try writing fiction. He went on to create two of the most notable series characters in Western pulp magazines. In 1936, Standard Magazines launched, and in *Texas Rangers,* Scott under the house name of **Jackson Cole** created Jim Hatfield, Texas Ranger, a character whose popularity was so great with readers that this magazine featuring his adventures lasted until 1958. When others eventually began contributing Jim Hatfield stories, Scott created another Texas Ranger hero,

Walt Slade, better known as *El Halcon,* the Hawk, whose exploits were regularly featured in *Thrilling Western.* In the 1950s Scott moved quickly into writing book-length adventures about both Jim Hatfield and Walt Slade in long series of original paperback Westerns. At the same time, however, Scott was also doing some of his best work in hardcover Westerns published by Arcadia House; thoughtful, well-constructed stories, with engaging characters and authentic settings and situations. Among the best of these, surely, are *Silver City* (1953), *Longhorn Empire* (1954), *The Trail Builders* (1956), and *Blood on the Rio Grande* (1959). In these hardcover Westerns, many of which have never been reprinted, Scott proved himself highly capable of writing traditional Western stories with characters who have sufficient depth to change in the course of the narrative and with a degree of authenticity and historical accuracy absent from many of his series stories.

We hope you have enjoyed this Large Print book. Other Thorndike, Wheeler, Kennebec, and Chivers Press Large Print books are available at your library or directly from the publishers.

For information about current and upcoming titles, please call or write, without obligation, to:

Publisher
Thorndike Press
295 Kennedy Memorial Drive
Waterville, ME 04901
Tel. (800) 223-1244

or visit our Web site at:

http://gale.cengage.com/thorndike

OR

Chivers Large Print
published by AudioGO Ltd
St James House, The Square
Lower Bristol Road
Bath BA2 3BH
England
Tel. +44(0) 800 136919
email: info@audiogo.co.uk
www.audiogo.co.uk

All our Large Print titles are designed for easy reading, and all our books are made to last.